"Why do you encourage h...

Kimberly's myriad worries came tumbling into her mind. "It's not good for her," she went on. "I don't want my aunt living in the past—"

"I do it because I'm fond of her, and my listening makes her happy," he said with the same intensity. "Ask me a better question—such as why I don't throttle you for sneaking into my room when the door is locked and pawing through my things. What did you think you'd find?"

His arms tightened round her. They felt safe and warm, yet she knew that with him, safety was an illusion. Kimberly gasped, half in pain and half in anticipation. "I don't know."

The wind rose again, wailing and making her shiver. "You're a maddening creature," he accused. "You've ransacked my room, you've stalked about all day ignoring me, and now you're trembling in my arms as if you could never be held closely enough."

Bethany Campbell, an English major and textbook consultant, calls her writing world her "hidey-hole," that marvelous place where true love always wins out. Her hobbies include writing poetry and thinking about that little scar on Harrison Ford's chin. She laughingly admits that her husband, who produces videos and writes comedy, approves of the first one only.

Books by Bethany Campbell

The Heart of the Sun

Bethany Campbell

Harlequin Books

TORONTO • NEW YORK • LONDON
AMSTERDAM • PARIS • SYDNEY • HAMBURG
STOCKHOLM • ATHENS • TOKYO • MILAN

ISBN 0-373-03045-2

Harlequin Romance first edition April 1990

To Dan,
who took me to Eureka.

CHAPTER ONE

IT WAS AN OMEN. There, among the leaves of the plum tree, sat the ghost-white squirrel.

Kimberly stopped. She stood, heart beating fast, on the path of quartz pebbles that meandered among the rose bushes.

She remembered what Beulah, the old woman who used to sell herbs and charms, had once told her. "When you see the white squirrel, you know that change is a-comin'. Life won't never be the same, girl, that's what seeing the white squirrel means."

She could not clearly see the animal. It was obscured by the branches of the plum tree, and it had gone as motionless as she had. Through the leaves it seemed to spy on her as intently as she tried to spy on it. Then, with a flick of its snowy tail, it vanished.

Change is coming, she thought superstitiously. Change is here. Things will never be the same.

The May breeze made the rose blossoms nod as in agreement. She shook her head in frustration. She had always known that the rare white animals lived in the mountains, as elusive as elves. As a child she had caught fleeting glimpses. Old Beulah's words about change meant nothing—life was always changing.

Except, the spring breeze seemed to say, stirring her long silky brown hair, everything *is* different this time. That she could not deny.

She had come home again because she had no choice. For two years she had been trying her luck as a commercial artist in Kansas City, and her luck had been bad. In love her luck had been even worse, if that were possible. A new art director named Roger Birch had been appointed to the ad agency at which she worked. He had arrived a month ago from Colorado, and Kimberly had immediately been taken with his brooding, burly charm.

He, in turn, seemed equally taken with her. He asked her out to little jazz places, took her for long walks in the park and to intimate little suppers in restaurants far from the main paths. She'd thought that at last her prince had arrived. The problem was that her prince didn't bother to inform her that he had a wife and two children. They were waiting in Colorado for their home to sell. Then they would join him.

When a co-worker told Kimberly the truth, at first she felt sick, and then enraged. She stormed into Roger's office, still carrying her freshly dipped paintbrush. "You're married," she had accused. He shrugged, as if it were a matter of small importance.

He calmly suggested she ignore the existence of his wife, his son, his daughter, and become his mistress. "We get along," he said. "I'll treat you right. I always like having somebody around the office."

Kimberly was never one to react mildly. She broke her paintbrush in two with a furious motion, flung the two pieces across his desk and quit on the spot. She left him sitting at his desk, his mouth open, a spot of fresh yellow-ocher paint dripping down his silk tie.

It had been an eloquent gesture but not exactly practical. She had no money saved, and there had been nothing to do but come home. She had tried to succeed in the great world and had failed on every level. It was as if all the family rumors of cursed love were true, and no Simpson woman would ever love happily. Perhaps it was her fate to return home, as if the house were an enchanted castle she was destined never to escape.

But even home was different now that her grandfather was dead. Aunt Dodo had showed unexpected enterprise by turning the eccentric house into a bed-and-breakfast inn. As an inn it was a qualified success. As a home it now left much to be desired.

Kimberly couldn't even be alone with her sorrows. She had arrived on Saturday and was sharing her bathroom with a lady from Boise, who gargled loudly for fifteen straight minutes every morning and evening. The woman also sang to herself. She was particularly fond of warbling "I'm a Little Teapot." It was not the best environment in which to nurse heartbreak and dashed career dreams.

In addition to the lady who warbled and gargled, there was the couple from the Middle West, whose idea of a fine vacation was to complain as much as possible. The bed in their first room was too soft, in their second, too hard. Aunt Dodo's delicious breakfasts were too fattening, and the tree frogs that sang all night long were too loud. If her grandfather, the colonel, had been alive, Kimberly thought wryly, he would have kicked them out with a mighty roar. The colonel had never been one to react mildly to anything, either.

But Aunt Dodo only blinked vaguely and went on doing what she had been doing all her life: trying to please.

Worst of all was the fourth guest, the man from Australia. The man from Australia bothered Kimberly. He was too good-looking, and that reminded her of the handsome art director, Roger, his deceit and his cold-blooded offer of adultery.

Like Roger, the man from Australia gave Kimberly long, disturbing looks that seemed to signal that the two of them shared some secret. She kept her manner icy, to tell him they shared nothing. Unlike Roger, he always seemed to be secretly amused at something, but she was in no mood for his deriding sideways smile. She was displeased to learn he was staying all summer.

He said he was a folklorist, collecting the old mountain stories and superstitions to compare them with those of the settlers in Australia and New Zealand. Something about his tall, tanned athletic body didn't look scholarly, though, and Kimberly instinctively distrusted him. She told her aunt so.

"Nonsense," Aunt Dodo had responded in her fluttering way. She had never distrusted anyone in her life. She hadn't had to. Grandfather, the colonel, had done enough distrusting for the entire family.

"Mr. Shaughnessy's a lovely man," Dodo insisted. "He's not like the other guests—he hasn't got a temperamental bone in his body. He has a refreshing joie de vivre and a pleasant curiosity about absolutely everything."

Kimberly thought Alec Shaughnessy had altogether too much curiosity, and she didn't find it pleasant. He made her uncomfortable, as if his mocking looks could strip her naked. His dark blue eyes missed nothing. They were so intent it was as if he were a magician, casting a spell on all around him. She wished he would go away and let her brood in peace.

She moved to the edge of the garden, peering down over the rock fence. The garden seemed to hang suspended in midair, the valley yawning beneath it. No house should exist among these sheer mountain peaks, no garden, no town. The entire little city of Eureka Springs, perched so improbably among the green steeps, seemed slightly unreal, like a conjurer's trick.

Light danced on the quartz in the low stone wall. Below, the mountainside fell away so sharply that it dizzied her to look. The town was built on these forbidding inclines because the forty-odd springs that flowed from the mountainsides were said to have special healing powers. People had flocked here for the miraculous waters. The springs were long ruined by civilization, but the town remained, a lure for tourists who fell in love with its airy eccentricity.

A town this odd, Kimberly philosophized, was probably a proper setting for a man as cranky and imperious as her grandfather. The colonel, a geologist, had built the house stone by stone when he left India and returned to America. He'd created a hanging garden on the mountainside almost by the sheer force of his ferocious will.

No two stones in the house were alike, nor were any cut or shaped by hand. The structure was a treasure trove of fossils and crystals and peculiar stones.

Other houses clung just as precipitously to the mountains. They were mostly ornately Victorian structures painted fanciful colors. But no house had the same magical air as this one. That was one thing that would never change.

Change, she thought restlessly, reminded of the spectral appearance of the white squirrel. So much had changed since the colonel died two years ago. Even in his old age he had been an impressive, handsome and autocratic man. The house was a small castle, and he had ruled it as absolutely as a king.

Except, she had learned, as king he had been as improvident as he had been willful. He had sold off the best of the family treasures bit by bit. At his death, little was left except the house, which, he'd told Aunt Dodo with his dying breath, she and Kimberly were never to relinquish.

Aunt Dodo, always obedient, was determined to keep the house in the family—even if it meant opening it to outsiders. Now it was full of strangers, and they seemed to Kimberly to crowd and jostle her thoughts, to swarm over her privacy and invade it. She wanted only to be alone. That was all—if she could just be alone to lick her wounds and recover.

"You shouldn't be alone on a morning this lovely," said a low, impertinent voice, slightly accented. "May I invade your privacy?"

Her heart leaped involuntarily. She turned, half-guiltily, and met the dark blue gaze of Alec Shaughnessy. He stood behind her, his sun-glazed hair tossing slightly in the breeze. She hadn't heard him approach.

"Invade away," she said with a casualness she did not feel. "When your house is an inn you don't have any privacy." She faced the valley again, trying to ignore Alec Shaughnessy. She felt him move beside her and gave him a quick, furtive glance.

He was tall, perhaps six feet, she calculated, a good nine inches taller than her own five-foot three. He was lean without being rangy.

Deeply tanned he was the kind of man whose hair would be dark in winter, gilded in summer. Now its brown thickness was streaked with such wide swaths of gold that he seemed blond. But his brows and lashes retained their darkness, and his mustache was brown, only faintly touched with the sun. His eyes, deep-set and alert, were such a hot electric blue she always met them with a slight shock.

The bronze of his tan was set off by the stark white of his short-sleeved shirt. He wore tight, faded jeans and white running shoes. He had long legs, and hips as flat and easy-moving as a cat's. He was a man designed to make a woman think dangerous thoughts.

"You don't sound very happy about it," Alec observed with a lazy laugh. "Playing hostess, that is. What's the matter? Has the family fortune dissipated? Fallen on hard times, have you?''

"You might say that," she returned noncommittally, darting another glance at him. He might be amused; she was not. Once more she was disconcerted by the contrasts in his face—the dark mustache and brows, the sun-streaked hair, the bronzed skin and ever-watchful blue eyes.

"Nothing to be ashamed of," he replied, leaning on the stone wall. "Some of the finest families in England do it— give tours of the ancestral castle. Even point out where the ghosts hang about. Have ghosts, do you?"

Sensing his scrutiny, Kimberly swallowed nervously. She resented him for making her feel edgy and prickly. She was supposed to be concentrating on her sorrows. "No ghosts," she answered curtly. Her tone said clearly that she didn't want to talk.

Alec ignored the unspoken message. He studied her for a long and agitating moment. She was small but compactly built and nicely curved. The ash-brown of her hip-length hair stirred sinuously in the breeze. The clear, faintly tanned skin, full pink lips and dark eyes were doubly striking with that mantle of shining hair. The line of her jaw was perhaps too stubborn for true beauty, but the spirit in her face eclipsed such a minor imperfection.

"Came out because I thought I saw a ghost myself," he offered, studying the obstinacy of her jawline carefully. "Could have sworn I saw a white squirrel. Gone daft, have I?" His gaze moved to her moist lips and rested there.

Impatiently she smoothed her long hair. "There was one here, yes. There are a few around."

"And?" he demanded, his mouth twisting upward slightly. He had an extremely disconcerting mouth, Kimberly thought in confusion.

Don't even think it, she scolded herself sternly. She was home because she'd been foolish enough to find a married man attractive. She recalled again the family story that a soothsayer in India had foretold that no woman in the Simpson family would ever love happily. So far it had proven eerily true. Men were best avoided.

"And so what," he drawled sarcastically, "does it mean?" The question forced her once more to meet his sapphire gaze.

"What do you mean, what does it mean?" she asked irritably.

"I mean," he said with a disarming smile, "certainly it must mean something to see a white squirrel. Everything in these mountains means something. If one sneezes on a Tuesday, it means something. Everything has a story or a superstition connected to it. That's why I'm here, you know. So what, pray, does a white squirrel *mean*?"

"Oh." She made a nonchalant gesture. "A change is coming into your life. That's all."

"A change?" Alec prodded, smiling. His smile was marvelous, and she had the feeling he knew and used it like a weapon. "That's a bit vague. What sort of change?"

"You'll have to ask the squirrel," she answered shortly. In some quirky way he was teasing her, and she didn't like it.

"Oh, I'm not that far gone, that I talk to squirrels," he protested with a derisive crook of his brow. "But we both saw the thing. So change will touch us both, eh?"

"If you believe the old stories," she said stiffly. She flexed her fingers, spreading them against the comforting solidity of the wall.

"Ah, yes. If you believe the old stories. Do you?" he taunted.

"Not particularly," she answered. "Look, all this is fascinating, but I've got to go. I'll leave you to your own devices. You can tie your kangaroo down or polish your boomerang or something."

He gave a slight snort of laughter. "Here!" he admonished. "Got a bit of a chip on your shoulder, haven't you? You ought to be nicer to your aunt's guests. She's working her heart out, you know."

"I think I can help her better in the kitchen than out here talking rodent lore," Kimberly replied with asperity. "Even albino rodent lore. So if you'll excuse me . . ."

She turned to go back to the house, but suddenly his body blocked her path. She found herself staring at the front of his snowy white shirt.

"I don't excuse you," he purred, crossing his bronzed arms. "Not yet. I want to know what makes the aunt so eager to please—but the niece so determined not to. Your aunt says you came home from Kansas City because you had job problems and a setback in love. Surely it was the job. A girl like you would never be luckless in love."

Kimberly bristled. She felt the blood surging to her cheeks. Her chest heaved slightly, and he watched the movement with admiring interest. She felt humiliated by his knowledge. Trust Dodo to tell everything to a stranger; Dodo was the most naive adult Kimberly knew.

He continued to study her, from the top of her brown hair to the ripe curves beneath her beige sweater and shorts, down to her smoothly tanned legs.

She flashed him a look of warning, but it seemed only to increase his self-satisfied insolence.

"My aunt shouldn't have told you anything," she accused. *My poor niece,* she could just imagine Dodo sighing wispily, *left her position because of advances from her em-*

ployer. Yes, Dodo would make it all sound positively nine-teenth century, even silly.

"I asked her," he stated, arching a brow. "I was curious why you came sweeping in last weekend, looking dramatic and slightly murderous. You do stalk about looking terribly dramatic, you know. Are you ever going to stop?"

"I'm not being dramatic," Kimberly said dramatically. "And I don't stalk." She started to stalk off.

His hands closed as firmly on her wrists as handcuffs, and he drew her back to stand before him on the path. She was surprised at the quickness and strength of his grasp. He released her almost immediately, but she stood there, too stunned to move away.

"There, there," he warned, his manner condescending. "If some man treated you poorly, he's a fool and not worth troubling yourself over. If it was the job that disturbed you, you should have stayed and found another. Or perhaps deep down, you wanted to come home, and used all this as an excuse. Have you actually sorted out your thoughts?"

"I'd *like* to sort them out," Kimberly rejoined sharply. "By myself. That's why I came home—to be alone, if you don't mind." But his odd observation bewildered her. Kimberly had never in her life been the kind to give up easily. Was he right? Had she really *wanted* to come home?

"Leave you alone?" he asked skeptically. "So you can feel sorry for yourself? You're not the type. Too full of fire. No, I think you came home because you missed this house—and knew your aunt needed help. She does, you know."

Kimberly didn't like the glint of superiority in his eyes. "My job was a joke, so I left it," she said defensively. "And if my aunt needs me, it's my business, not yours."

His mouth twisted in wry disbelief, and his mustache twisted with it. "Sorry," he said sarcastically. "Just making an observation. A job isn't a joking matter. It's self-indulgent to walk off from one—unless your heart draws you elsewhere so strongly you can't say no."

"Keep your observations," Kimberly answered defiantly. He was confusing her, forcing her onto paths of thought she didn't want to travel. She had long suspected that Dodo needed her here, and when she'd arrived, her suspicions were confirmed. She needed time to sort all these problems out, to put them in perspective. "My aunt and I are no concern of yours," she told him.

"But you are. Because . . ." He bent closer, smiling, but there was no mirth in his smile. For a split second all his easy charm seemed to vanish. He seemed as polished and dangerous as a knife blade. But then the playfulness sparkled in his eyes again, the slant of his mouth softened, and Kimberly was unsure of what she'd seen in that unguarded second.

"Because?" she asked, suddenly wary. Her anger vanished, replaced by something close to fear.

"Because," he replied, nodding with mock solemnity. "Because I like your aunt. I like this place, this house. I intend to spend the summer. And I don't want to suffer the moods and pouts and tempers of a sulky adolescent."

"I'm not an adolescent," Kimberly answered stiffly. "I'm twenty. An adult. I'll thank you to treat me like one." Again she tried to walk away, and again she felt his hand clamping around her wrist.

"Then act like one," he ordered. Again the laughter disappeared momentarily from his eyes. "Being twenty doesn't make you the queen of all knowledge. Understand?" He gave her arm a slight but jarring shake. "Nor does it give you the right to inflict your moods on everyone else—especially me. This may be your home, but it's also an inn. And I'm a paying guest."

She stared up at him distrustfully.

He merely smiled. With a slight flourish he released her, then thrust his hands into his pockets. "Now," he said, "sit down, will you?" He nodded toward the white wrought iron seat that encircled the catalpa tree at the garden's center.

She rubbed her wrist. In doubt and confusion she stood absolutely still, watching the sunlight gleam on his streaked hair. To march away would prove to him that he was right, that she was childish and moody. To obey him, however, seemed merely to let him win in another way.

"All right." He shrugged, gazing down at her. "Don't sit. Just talk—civilly. Tell me, for instance, what kind of job is such a joke that you took the luxury of walking away from it?"

A job in which your superior is a lying snake trying to get you into his bed, Kimberly thought bitterly, *and worse, he almost did.* But she wasn't about to tell Alec Shaughnessy. Instead she answered him in the kind of mocking tone he could understand.

"This job," she asserted, looking up grimly into his sardonic face, "was a joke, all right. For a year and a half I tried to get full-time work as an artist. Kansas City's full of starving artists—believe me, I was one. Six months ago I finally got a job with the Damler Ad Agency. I spent the last half year drawing dancing mustard jars. And that, Mr. Shaughnessy, is a joke. Not a particularly good one, but a joke. On me."

"Dancing mustard jars?" he asked dubiously.

"I worked on the Mussfarber Mustard account. I worked *only* on the Mussfarber Mustard account. For six months I tried to draw a mustard jar that danced the way Mr. Mussfarber imagined a mustard jar should dance. I drew mustard jars that waltzed. I drew mustard jars that polkaed. I drew mustard jars that tap-danced and did the highland fling. I drew every kind of dancing mustard jar in the world—except the kind that Mr. Mussfarber wanted but couldn't describe.''

The dark brows drew together in a frown. ''Dancing mustard jars?'' he said again, as if the thought were intrinsically painful.

''Yes,'' she agreed blackly. ''On a really good day I was allowed to draw a hamburger or a hotdog dancing *with* the mustard jar. But they were never what Mr. Mussfarber wanted, either. It was not the most fulfilling job in the world.''

''I should think not,'' he answered, his expression ironic. ''Slave to the mustard moguls of the world—certainly no job for a woman of artistic temperament. I see your point.''

''Thank you,'' she said sweetly. ''And now that you know all my dark and mustardy secrets, may I go? If it doesn't offend your guestship?''

He gave her a wry look that made her feel approximately two inches tall. ''Steady,'' he said, raising one lean hand in warning. ''I fear you've spent too much time among the spices. Like mustard, you have a bite. I don't know all your secrets. Are you going to tell me about the man? Your superior, I think your aunt said. And do you really imagine that he's broken your heart and sent you, weeping, here?''

Again his easy smile seemed to conceal something. She thought she detected a strange intensity in his eyes. ''The man,'' she said, her words clipped, ''doesn't matter. He's none of your business.''

''If you continue to take your anger with him out on me, he is,'' Alec objected. ''But I'll pry no more. I know the most important thing about you and him, anyway.''

''What?'' she asked defiantly. He was the most audacious man she'd ever met, the last sort of person she needed to meet after Roger had shattered her emotions.

Alec laughed. He touched the tip of her nose. "You've got the slightest cleft in the tip of your nose," he said. "Just like your aunt. Did you know? It's charming."

His movement was so quick it startled her. His hands could move as swiftly as those of a magician.

"I don't know what the tip of my nose has to do with anything." She rubbed her nose irritably as if to scrub away the memory of his touch. The motion made her sneeze, a small sneeze.

"Bless you," he said, with his never-ending cocksure smile. "You've sneezed on Tuesday. I suppose you don't know what that means, either. 'Sneeze on Monday, sneeze for danger; sneeze on Tuesday, kiss a stranger'—an old folk rhyme in these hills. An accurate one, I'm told. You may soon kiss a stranger."

The possibility rattled her, made her steal a glance at his curved mouth. She caught herself and gave him a cool look. "I doubt it," she said pertly. "Collect as many superstitions as you like, Mr. Shaughnessy—just don't make the mistake of believing them. Will you excuse me now?"

She gave him a smile of counterfeit sugar and honey, then turned on her heel and walked briskly back to the stone house.

"For now," he called after her pleasantly. "For now."

Alec Shaughnessy stood looking after her. Damn, he thought, she was too sharp by half, full of ginger she was, and beautiful to boot. It was bad luck she'd come home. The aunt he could handle. The aunt was child's play.

But the girl was another story. She had been hurt in love, and it made her suspicious. He didn't need a suspicious woman around. And the only way he knew to turn a suspicious woman into a trusting one was to make her fall in love. He found that cynical piece of knowledge disturbing, for she was a lovely little thing who didn't need hurting again.

Still, he would not let the girl with the flashing dark eyes stand in his way. He would beguile her however he could. He would do whatever he had to. But still, the darkness of her eyes and that thick veil of silky hair made him uneasy, on edge.

"DON'T," Kimberly insisted firmly, "tell that smirking man anything else about me. I mean it."

Aunt Dodo looked at her with large violet-blue eyes. "Oh, dear." Her voice quavered guiltily. "I didn't mean to anger you, Kimberly. It's just that he seemed so interested—and he's such an engaging man. I thought that after that unfortunate business in Kansas City—"

Dodo looked so wounded that Kimberly reached out and took the mixing bowl from her to show her aunt that she still loved her. She channeled her anger into ferociously stirring the pancake batter.

"*I* don't think he's engaging," Kimberly muttered grimly. "Besides, I don't trust 'engaging' men. They're usually hiding something."

"Oh!" mourned Dodo, casting her great eyes heavenward. "You sound so cynical! One must never be cynical, Kimberly. It numbs the soul, simply numbs it."

"The soothsayer in India was right," Kimberly grumbled with all the cynicism she could raise, and stirred harder still. "Love is never going to work for the women in this family. So spare me any matchmaking."

"How could you remember the soothsayer in India?" Dodo asked, her soft face puzzled. "You weren't even born. I don't even remember it, not quite."

"Grandfather and you both told me. Half a hundred times," Kimberly answered, exasperated.

"Yes, well..." Dodo said vaguely and flicked an imaginary speck from one of her apron's numerous frills. "Well, maybe it just applied to your mother and me—not to you."

Kimberly sighed. She knew little of her mother's marriage except that it had been rebellious, brief and disastrous. Her mother had come home barely a year later, asking humbly for the colonel's forgiveness. She had died of peritonitis when Kimberly was only five. Kimberly could barely remember her. In her pictures she was a small, slim woman with a jaw that was both fragile and stubborn, and dark, haunted eyes.

"No," Kimberly said, squaring her shoulders. "I wasn't meant to fall in love. And I don't like that man, so please don't talk to him about me."

"But, dear," Dodo said plaintively in pretty frustration, "what if he asks? I can't just be rude!"

Good grief, Kimberly thought hopelessly, how had Dodo even managed to start herself in the innkeeping business, much less succeed at it? "Tell him," she said between her teeth, "that *I* won't like it if you talk about me."

"Oh," murmured Dodo, light breaking across her face. "Of course. Why didn't I think of that? Goodness, where's the syrup? Did I give you the syrup, Kimberly?"

"You already set it out," Kimberly said, smiling in spite of herself. She put down the bowl of pancake batter, moved into the dining room and began setting the table.

"Of course," Dodo nodded, musing. "I remember.... Father always said I was a flibbertigibbet, and I am! I am! Excuse me, dear, but my entrepreneurial endeavors have taxed my brain to its limit. But not to worry—Mr. Shaughnessy won't hear another word about you through these lips—tick-lock! Shut tight!" She pretended to lock her rosebud mouth, then threw away the imaginary key.

Kimberly shook her head as she laid out the silver. It was impossible to remain angry at Dodo. It was like trying to focus resentment on a butterfly. She decided to change the subject.

"Dodo," she asked thoughtfully, "what do the mountain people say it means if you have a little cleft in the tip of your nose?"

"Mercy!" exclaimed Dodo, her grey curls tossing and her large eyes widening. "Whyever do you ask *that*?"

"I'm just asking," Kimberly said, nonplussed at her aunt's reaction. "What's it mean?"

"Why," Dodo replied, her voice dropping to a stage whisper, "a slight cleft on the nose means that a woman's a—a virgin, that's what. They say it disappears as soon as a girl—well, you know. Hush! Someone will hear us talking of such things."

Dodo touched the tiny indentation at the tip of her own nose almost reverently. Then she squinted at Kimberly. She adjusted her thick glasses and squinted even harder.

Kimberly realized that she was being examined for the telltale sign of purity. She blushed. She remembered Alec Shaughnessy touching the tip of her nose less than half an hour ago, saying he knew the most important thing about her unfortunate relationship with Roger.

She blushed harder. Alec was right. She hadn't slept with Roger. For this, she thanked her stars. She might be cursed in love, but at least she wasn't *that* cursed. She rubbed at the tip of her nose self-consciously.

She covered her mouth quickly, for once more the motion made her sneeze. The perturbing words echoed in her brain, "Sneeze on Tuesday, kiss a stranger."

She wasn't going to kiss a stranger, she told herself furiously. She wasn't going to kiss anybody. She thought of Roger, kissing her so softly and lingeringly. She felt slightly sick. The memory of his dark, square face filled her with shame. To think she had loved such a man. She would never get over it, she told herself sternly. Never. She would probably suffer forever.

CHAPTER TWO

PERCHED TIPSILY atop the steepest part of the Ozark Mountains, Eureka Springs was one of the most improbable towns in North America. Located just south of the Missouri border, it resembled a small and fanciful Switzerland. Tourists descended by the tens of thousands to enjoy its picturesque beauty, its wealth of shops and galleries, its ornate Victorian hotels.

Its streets were so steep and curving that no two simply intersected. Instead they coiled, curled, climbed, intertwined, looped, doubled back and merged. So sheer were the heights on which the houses were built that a man might look out his back door and straight down into his neighbor's chimney. Instead of a backyard, a house might have a chasm.

Built where no town was ever meant to be built, the city had made peculiar concessions to the mountains. The Catholic church was nestled against a mountain so steep, no room was left available for a front entrance to the building. To enter, one climbed the twisting road and walked in through the steeple.

Kimberly, long used to these oddities, trotted agilely down the tumbling sheerness of Spring Street. She carried a bundle of small, framed watercolors.

Yesterday she had gone from shop to shop on the Basin Park Hotel side of the street, trying to talk shopkeepers into placing a few of her fanciful landscapes among their stores' wares. Competition was fierce, since Eureka was filled to the brim with artists of every sort.

Today she worked the Palace Hotel side of the street. So far, after six stores, she had placed paintings only in two. She decided to stop at the little sidewalk café beside the hotel and brace herself with a tall glass of iced tea.

Calvin, the town's most durable folk singer, sat on an orange crate near the curb, serenading the world as it passed by. He accompanied himself on an antique mandolin inlaid with mother-of-pearl. His straw hat was on the sidewalk in front of him, as if politely asking passersby for a contribution to keep the concern going.

Calvin liked to pretend he was something of a scoundrel, but Kimberly knew he was at heart merely harmless, friendly and entertaining. She dropped fifty cents into his hat. "Stop and have a drink with me," she said.

"Are you buying?" Calvin asked cagily, staring up at her through his spectacles. His curly gray hair puffed out over his ears, but the top of his head gleamed baldly in the sun. He had a sumptuous gray mustache and was dressed in well-pressed gray trousers, red suspenders, and a T-shirt that said Support Your Local Troubadour.

"I just gave you fifty cents," Kimberly protested. "Besides, you're working, and I'm not."

"All right, already," Calvin agreed. "Order me a beer. But give me a minute. I see tourist dollars puffing up the street." Calvin began to pick a melody from his mandolin, and his reedy voice floated on the sunny air.

Kimberly sat down and leaned back in her chair to watch the performance. Calvin's song vibrated with the most mournful of mountain accents, as if generations of pure Southern hill-folk had produced his voice. This was a good trick, since Calvin was from Pasadena, California and had never set foot in the South until he was over forty.

Calvin, however, was an excellent folk singer, even if he had learned all of his songs out of library books and not at his dear old granny's knee. He didn't mind a bit if tourists mistook him for a native product; indeed his livelihood depended on it.

His ruse worked, as usual. The tourists he had spotted rained a shower of coins into the waiting hat. As soon as they passed, he scooped up the money, put his hat on his balding head and joined Kimberly.

"So, sweet Kim," he said, his Southern accent vanished. "Did you see the size of that donation? Here. Take your fifty cents back. Your money's no good around here. And I'll buy." They placed their order with a passing waiter.

"You're incorrigible," Kimberly warned, turning back to Calvin, but she smiled. "I never know what to make of you. A real gentleman and an artificial hillbilly."

He twirled his gray mustache. "There are hardly any real hillbillies left," he said glibly. "They all moved to the city. They play video games nowadays, not banjos. Somebody has to give the public what it wants. And I'm an accommodating guy. So what brings you home? Finally give up on the city?"

"The city gave up on me," Kimberly said wryly. "My job was no good, my new boss was vile, so I quit—and here I am." The history of my life and love for the past two years, she thought, and it could be put in one sentence.

Calvin twined a curl of his gray hair thoughtfully. "I'll bet there's more to it than that," he hazarded. "I'll bet there's a romance gone bad in there somewhere. I'd bet another round of drinks on it."

"No bets," Kimberly murmured unhappily. Maybe it showed after all, that she'd been lied to, trifled with and betrayed.

"So you've come home, your heart broken," offered Calvin. "How tragic. Maybe I'll sing about it. 'Love, O, love, O careless love...'"

Kimberly tossed him an unappreciative look. She wanted to feel sorry for herself, and Calvin was making it impossible. "My heart *was* broken," she asserted indignantly. "At least it feels like it. You shouldn't make fun. Besides, I'm out of work, too."

"So help out your aunt," Calvin said, unimpressed. "She's got the potential for a nice little business there, if she had some dependable help. You could help her turn a tidy profit on that weird old pile of rocks."

Kimberly shook her head hopelessly. "Calvin, that weird old pile of rocks is my house. My grandfather built it. Is nothing sacred to you?"

He stuck his hand in his pocket so that the coins jingled merrily. "Yeah," he said with a venal grin. "Money. Your grandfather certainly isn't. Or wasn't. He was an old tyrant. It's a marvel that Dodo's bounced back the way she has. She seems positively outgoing these days."

"Yes." Kimberly sighed, remembering how her aunt had spent so many years as nearly a recluse, caring for the possessive colonel. "At least there's that. I don't know how she does it. She can be so—so vague sometimes."

"Oh, Dodo's more capable than anybody ever gives her credit for," Calvin said sagely. He stroked one tip of his sweeping mustache. "But she needs help. It's good you're back."

Kimberly nodded guiltily and sipped her tea. Dodo seemed impossibly soft and fluttery, but she had somehow always managed to do whatever had to be done, no matter how difficult. This innkeeping business, though, was too much for a woman her age. Kimberly should have realized it sooner.

"The Aussie's been asking about you all, you know," Calvin said. He took off his hat and ran his hand over his gleaming pate. "Just thought I'd mention it."

Kimberly looked at him in confusion. "Who? What?" she asked. "Who was asking about who?"

Calvin pushed his glasses down on his nose and peered at her. "Your new resident—Mr. Alec Shaughnessy. He was asking about your grandfather."

Kimberly frowned, immediately alert. There were many stories about her grandfather, few of them flattering. But none of them should be any business of Mr. Shaughnessy's. "Why?"

"I don't know," Calvin said, his pale eyes studying her dark ones. "It began innocently enough. He bought me a couple of beers last night and started asking me about folklore. As I say, I try to be accommodating."

Kimberly gave him a satirical glance. "You mean you fooled him? He thought you grew up here? For shame, Calvin. What do you know about folklore?"

He pushed his glasses back into place haughtily. "I know a lot. I read books. I used to talk to Old Beulah—she knew it all. This is my business, you know, hanging around looking like a genuine home-grown product. And no, I didn't fool him. Halfway through the first beer, just when I was getting going, he looks at me and says in that accent, 'You've read all this somewhere, haven't you, you old devil? You're not from around here.' Then he smiled like a *young* devil."

Kimberly felt a peculiar frisson. Alec Shaughnessy had grace, charm, striking good looks. But most of all, he had intelligence. It shone out of his eyes like light. Perhaps that was what made him seem both dangerous and intriguing.

"So," Calvin said, sipping his beer, "we keep talking, sort of scholar to scholar. I give him all the information I've stolen here and there."

And that, thought Kimberly ruefully, is probably where Alec Shaughnessy got his embarrassing observation on how to tell a virgin by the tip of her nose.

"A few beers later, and he starts asking about local history," Calvin continued. "A few beers later still, the conversation drifts around to your grandfather and some of the rumors about him and that house of yours—"

"Oh, no," Kimberly protested in disgust. "Calvin, you didn't tell him those old stories—that grandfather built that house to hide a fortune in gems from India—you didn't, did you?"

"Well," Calvin shrugged lamely. "I know it's just a story, but it's a *good* story. And by that time I had two young devils to entertain, because I was seeing double. You know I'm a ham, Kimberly. Give me a good audience and I can't stop myself."

Kimberly set down her iced tea. Despite the beating sun, she was no longer thirsty. "Why," she demanded, "would he be interested in grandfather and those old rumors? I thought he was here to compare our folk tales and superstitions to Australia's."

"So did I," Calvin muttered. "I started wondering myself this morning—when my hangover let me. Nobody's drunk me under the table in twenty years. But he did. And while he was doing it, it was your family he wanted to know about."

Kimberly tried to shake off her apprehension. "Maybe it's just because he's staying in the house," she murmured. "Because he knows Dodo, and she's probably told him about the colonel. That's probably all it is."

"Maybe," Calvin said noncommittally. "Maybe."

She gave him a long appraising look, cocking one wing-like brow. "Just what did you tell him?" she asked.

Calvin grinned, showing his strong white teeth. "That's a good question, baby cakes, because I don't quite remember."

Kimberly looked heavenward in frustration. "You don't remember?"

"Look on the bright side," Calvin urged and finished his beer. "If I don't know the truth, I make it up. I probably added ten more rumors to your family mythology. He won't know what to believe. Ah, the drama of it all. What a master thespian I would have made."

"Calvin," Kimberly muttered out of the side of her mouth. "Have you no sense of responsibility? Of loyalty?"

"Not much," he said with disconcerting honesty. "At least not when the beer is free."

"Please, please, *please* don't tell this man anything else about my family. He's an outsider. It's none of his business." She lowered her thick lashes, narrowing her eyes. "If not for me, then for Dodo's sake," she said craftily. She had always suspected that Calvin, for all his cynicism, had a soft spot for Dodo. They were close to the same age, and Dodo always had been and always would be a beautiful woman. She could have had her share of conquests if the colonel would have allowed it.

"My brains were addled by brew," Calvin countered, maintaining his innocence. "But sure. Just tell me if one thing is true or not."

"What?" she asked, looking at his curling tufts of hair, springing gray mustache and insouciant smile.

He leaned closer, conspiratorially. "Did some Hindu fakir really put a curse on the women in your family? So that none of you would ever be happy in love?"

"Certainly not," Kimberly said with disdain. She wasn't precisely lying. It had been a soothsayer, not a fakir, and it had been more of a prophesy than an actual curse, although maybe somewhere there was a curse involved.

"Oh," Calvin said, staring at his empty beer bottle with regret. "Too bad. But it still makes a good story."

"Only," Kimberly told him dryly, "if it isn't about you. Adieu, Calvin. I've got to go try to peddle some pictures."

"And I must pluck my mandolin and warble my counterfeit woodnotes wild. Ah," he sighed philosophically, "the artist's life is not an easy one. So long, toots. Tell your aunt not to work too hard. Maybe I'll come see the two of you sometime."

She smiled, gathered her paintings and started up the street again, dodging the crowds of tourists. Behind her she could hear Calvin singing.

"Love, O love, O careless love,

O, see what love has done to me..."

She hurried onward. The words of the song bit into her. Her love had been both careless and painful. She should have known Calvin would be irreverent about everything—including her fractured romance.

But why, she wondered, did the charming old fraud have to tell everything he knew about her family to Alec Shaughnessy? And why was Alec asking, anyway?

She knew there were wild rumors of hidden wealth connected with her grandfather's years in India, but none of them was true, or she and Dodo would not now be nearly as poor as church mice. Besides, the colonel's time in India was decades ago, before she was born, before even Alec Shaughnessy was born.

The old stories should have nothing to do with her. Nor should they have anything to do with a stranger, whose eyes were bluer than any jewels that had ever shone beneath the mystic Indian sky.

"A GLASS of sherry, Mr. Shaughnessy?" Dodo asked. She was hovering about the front porch like a hummingbird.

"Only if you sit down and join us," Alec replied firmly. "You work too hard by half, my girl. Sit down and tell Mrs. Munroe about the house. It's a fascinating story."

"Oh, *yes*!" caroled Lela Munroe enthusiastically. She was the new guest. "Sit down, Miss Simpson. You mustn't wait on us hand and foot this way."

No, Kimberly thought, Dodo shouldn't be waiting on everyone so devotedly. This offer of wine and sherry to guests in the evening was going beyond the call of duty. Kimberly had spent the day helping her aunt tidy up the rooms after departing guests to make ready for this new one, Lela Munroe, a woman of thirty, just separated from her husband.

Lela Munroe's eyes had fastened on Alec Shaughnessy with hungry fascination as soon as she'd seen him. She seemed determined to spend the evening by his side. She was a bosomy woman with flyaway blond hair and a patronizing air.

Dodo treated her royally, which Lela Munroe relished. Dodo was working entirely too hard, Kimberly thought worriedly. She looked positively worn this evening. Calvin was right—it was good Kimberly had come home.

She took the tray with the glasses and decanters from her aunt. She made Dodo sit in the big cobra-backed wicker chair and poured her a thimbleful of sherry.

Feeling Alec Shaughnessy's watchful blue eyes on her, she poured herself a glass as well. She sat down on the porch swing, folding her legs under her carefully. She had changed out of her shorts and into a simple pink sundress.

Alec had spent the day, he said, tracking down the town's oldest residents to talk about the lore of the hills. He sat easily in the other cobra-backed chair, his hair looking almost dark as the evening shadows fell. He wore hip-hugging gray slacks, a gray chambray work shirt, and calf-high boots of polished black leather.

Across the dusty porch, he smiled at Kimberly slightly, one corner of his mouth crooking up under his mustache. She ignored him.

"Your father built this house entirely by himself?" Lela Munroe asked Dodo. "What an individualist he must have been!" Kimberly suspected Lela Munroe cared little about the house, only wished to play up to Alec's interest in it.

But Dodo brightened. She loved to talk about the colonel. He had been, after all, the center of her life. "Oh, yes," she agreed with her wispy, nostalgic voice. "My father was a great individualist—he led a most unusual life." She took a tiny sip of sherry and cast a worried look at Alec Shaughnessy. She blinked her large violet eyes. "But I don't want to bore Mr. Shaughnessy by telling the same old stories again," she objected apologetically.

Alec gave her his most beguiling smile. "Miss Simpson, my business is listening to the same stories retold again and again. It's a business I love. Tell Mrs. Munroe. I insist."

"Well," Dodo murmured, looking pleased, "if you're certain, Mr. Shaughnessy." She turned to Lela Munroe. Lela smiled at Alec as if to say, "Isn't the fussy old dear cute?"

The evening breeze stirred Dodo's gray curls. She held the stem of her sherry glass delicately. "The colonel—my father—was a gemologist and geologist," she began reverently. "His military title was bestowed in Brazil, when he advised the government about the emerald mines. His work took him everywhere—but it was India that he loved most...."

Kimberly settled dreamily against the cushions of the porch swing. She knew Dodo's story by heart. The years in India had obviously been the most fabulous in Dodo's life—and in the colonel's as well. But it had been all so long ago, so far away, it seemed to Kimberly to have happened in a land of myth. What difference did it all make now?

She tried to stretch discreetly, to stifle a small yawn. But then her eyes met those of Alec Shaughnessy, and she was jarred back into wakeful awareness. He sat, long legs crossed, his boots gleaming darkly in the sun's last rays.

He was listening to Dodo, but his gaze never left Kimberly. A sort of unspoken electric challenge crackled between them. She thought he gave her his taunting ghost of a smile but could not be sure in the fading light.

She looked away and stared out into the thick scarlet blossoms of the flowering quince. But when she stole another look at him, her skin prickled. He still stared at her, coolly, boldly and without apology.

"Oh, India!" Dodo was rhapsodizing. "It was near the end of the Raj—the British rule—and never again will the world see such splendor. My father was hired by the Rajah of Bholapur to oversee his gem prospecting and purchasing. Bholapur was said to have great resources in both diamonds and garnets. And the maharaja was mad for jewels—we lived as his guests at his palace for two years, and my sister and I were treated like princesses..."

"As well you might be, Miss Simpson," Alec Shaughnessy said gallantly. He drained his glass as if in salute.

Dodo started to rise to refill his glass, but he shook his head. Obediently she folded her hands in the lap of her ruffled apron. "Go on, Miss Simpson," Alec commanded gently. "Don't let me interrupt your intriguing reminiscences."

He rose from his chair, uncoiling his length with silent, almost feline grace. He stepped to the little wicker table and refilled his glass. A lock of gilded hair fell over his forehead.

"Some people criticized the rajah," Dodo said in her soft, almost childlike voice. "He was certainly the most rebellious prince in all of India—but to us he was ever the perfect gentleman."

Alec set down the sherry decanter. Instead of returning to his seat, he strolled to the porch railing, next to the swing where Kimberly sat. He leaned against the white pillar, crossing his long, booted legs. He hooked one thumb over his belt.

In the deepening shadows his face looked dark and hawklike. Kimberly sensed rather than saw his keen eyes resting on her once more. She shifted uncomfortably and tried to concentrate her attention on Dodo, who suddenly looked frail and wistful to her.

"His name was Rajah Udit Krishmaja Rawal," Dodo said with fond remembrance, "and he had never really accepted the rule of the British. Oh, he was a proud man—and a mighty one. The British wanted him to admit certain companies to mine copper, but he would never agree! For he was the rajah, and it pleased him to look for jewels instead. And I suppose he rather enjoyed making such a fuss over us, the mere Americans. He positively enjoyed spiting the British advisor."

"Perhaps," Alec suggested silkily, "you should explain to Mrs. Munroe precisely what the advisor was."

Casually he stepped away from the porch pillar and settled onto the cushioned swing beside Kimberly. She had sat as still as a wary mouse. But now he used one booted foot to lever the swing into slow and rhythmic motion. Back and forth it went, almost hypnotically.

Kimberly sucked in her breath. She had curled up in the swing, her legs folded on the white cushions. Now her knees nearly touched the muscular thighs of Alec Shaughnessy. There was something disturbing about his nearness, something oddly unnerving in the slow rhythmic motion he had initiated.

"Oh, of course," Dodo mused, not even noticing that Alec had moved next to her niece. She smiled at Lela Munroe. Lela pretended to listen avidly, but her eyes kept jealous track of Alec.

"The British advisor," Dodo continued. "Well, the rajah had clashed with every advisor the Crown appointed. And so Sir Cyril Damon was sent—a man as headstrong as the rajah himself. He threatened to have the rajah removed from the throne and replaced by the rajah's cousin, Pratap, who was much easier to control."

"My goodness," gushed Mrs. Munroe with what sounded like false enthusiasm, "a power struggle for a throne—and you were actually *there*. How exciting!"

Dodo nodded solemnly, her violet eyes wide. "Oh, it was a wonderful and terrifying place," she said. "And more than one maharaja lost his rule and was replaced by someone more cooperative—yet the Rajah of Bholapur was a man of *such* influence and power that he was treated very carefully until Sir Cyril came. From the first my father predicted it would end badly, and he was right."

"Your father had a remarkable insight into human nature," Alec Shaughnessy drawled. Kimberly thought she detected the slightest trace of sarcasm in his voice. She slid him a sideways glance, but as she did so, he stretched languidly and placed his arm along the back of the swing.

For the briefest of moments, his knuckles brushed the nape of her neck, and her body went first cold then warm. She was sure his touch had been studied and purposeful. Yet he himself did not seem to have noticed. Now his arm was so near her shoulders that she could actually feel the heat of his sun-bronzed skin.

Dodo leaned forward, like an earnest young girl, her hands folded in her lap. "The trouble erupted at last over a jewel—a great jewel. Sir Cyril practically ordered the rajah to allow the mining of copper. The rajah even accepted fabulous sums of money for mineral rights from certain British companies. But then, just to show he was the rajah, he turned around and refused to let them come in—and he spent their money on what was to be the most extraordinary jewel in his collection, one of the largest red-gold topazes ever mined. He bought it before it was even cut—a stone of twelve thousand carats."

"Twelve thousand carats!" squeaked Lela Munroe, dropping all pretense of politeness. "Did you say twelve thousand carats? That can't be right. That's impossible."

"Oh," Dodo murmured, sounding unnerved by the challenge, "but it was real—I saw it myself."

"Twelve thousand carats," sniffed Lela Munroe suspiciously. She tossed Alec a conspiratorial look. "You were only a child when all this happened. Your memory is playing tricks."

Alec's cool voice took momentary charge of the conversation. "Miss Simpson isn't mistaken," he said with quiet authority. "Such stones exist. Cut, the thing would be considerably smaller, of course. Probably about six thousand carats. The Royal Ontario Museum has a topaz twice that large—colorless, though."

Kimberly tensed at his voice, so velvety, so confident and so close to her ear. "I didn't know you were an expert on gems, Mr. Shaughnessy," she said. She allowed herself to look at him boldly. "I thought your area of specialization was folklore."

He shifted slightly, facing her. His arm touched the back of her neck once again, so briefly she almost thought she imagined it. "I know nothing about gems," he replied, a soft taunt in his voice. "When your aunt first told me the story, I read up on them in the encyclopedia in the den. It's no sin for a man to be curious, surely."

Then in the darkness, she felt his hand momentarily cup the silky curve of her bare shoulder. She shuddered away from his touch.

"It depends on what the man is curious about," Kimberly countered, a chill in her voice. But again she was uncertain. She was sure she had felt his touch, sudden, warm and presumptuous. At least she thought she was sure. But he gave no indication he had touched her at all. Or that if he had, it had been anything but accidental.

"A topaz of six thousand carats sounds ludicrous to me," grumbled Lela Munroe. She obviously no longer found Dodo's story believable and wondered why Alec cared. "It wouldn't even be pretty. A person couldn't even wear it."

"Oh, no," Dodo breathed in awe, clearly recalling fables of the gem. "One wouldn't wear it, of course. It's a piece for a collection—but once cut, it would be more beautiful than you can imagine. Especially that color—like a piece of the sunset. Oh, I saw many a jewel in India—the court was filled with jewels—but never a jewel like that. It was the only one of its kind. It came from South America. It was called the Heart of the Sun."

"Well," muttered Lela Munroe, looking critically at her own diamonds, which must have seemed suddenly paltry, "I can't blame everyone for being upset with the rajah. He as good as stole the money from investors, then turned around and bought himself a bauble with it.''

"But,'' Dodo said, sounding eager to communicate the importance of the idea, ''he was the rajah—don't you see? To him, it was a perfectly acceptable thing to do—to show that no one could dictate to him. I'm not saying it was right. But from his point of view, it wasn't *wrong*. Of course, the British advisor didn't see it that way.''

"I wouldn't blame the advisor if he'd pushed the old rajah right off his throne,'' Lela Munroe said righteously.

Dodo suddenly looked weary and sorrowful. "Very few people would have blamed the advisor if he had replaced the rajah,'' Dodo said, her voice trembling. "But he didn't replace him. He took his life. He killed him. And stole the Heart of the Sun.''

"Good God!'' said Lela Munroe. She looked at Dodo, so small, proper and soft-spoken, the relic of another era. Without asking, Lela reached to the table and poured herself a stiff dollop of sherry. "He actually *killed* him? Was he tried? Was he punished? Did they find the jewel?''

Dodo nodded sadly. "He was tried. He was not convicted. The evidence, the court said, was too flimsy. He was destroyed anyway, sadly. His own family had invested heavily in the copper mines of Bholapur, which was quite wrong for them to do—no wonder Sir Cyril was enraged with the rajah. But the jewel was never recovered. Sir Cyril left India in disgrace and migrated to Canada—they say. He most certainly took the jewel with him. His family fortune, after all, was ruined, as was his reputation. As for my father, well his heart was almost broken.''

"Because of what happened to this Sir Cyril?'' Lela Munroe asked, then drank half her sherry at a gulp. She obviously found the story bizarre but did not know how to compete with it.

"No," Dodo stated simply. "Because of the rajah. Father said he was the best friend he ever had—the most generous, independent and fearless. But he was replaced by his cousin Pratap. And we came back to America. I have never seen India since." Regret trembled in Dodo's voice. "But I'll never forget it," she said softly. "Never. We were treated like princesses, my sister and I."

"Hmmmph," observed Lela. She obviously felt upstaged by the tale. "How odd, to come from this little town, see the whole world and live with a rajah—and then to come right back where you started."

"Oh, we didn't start from here," Dodo explained. "The colonel was shattered by events in India. We came here because nobody knew us. And because geologically it is an interesting area with so many kinds of stones—gems, too. As a sort of therapy, he built this house. He chose every stone himself. And no two are alike. Each is unique."

Dodo babbled on happily, talking of the house's oddities, and Kimberly sat silently, not listening to her aunt. During the familiar recitation, all she'd been aware of was the disturbing nearness of Alec Shaughnessy.

The heat of his muscular arm draped behind her seemed to radiate through her, filling her body with warm tickling. His fingertips rested tantalizingly near her bare shoulder, not quite making contact. Although he didn't touch her, his closeness surrounded her like a sensual cloud.

The scent of his bay rum wafted to her, dizzying her slightly. If she stole a sideways glance at him, she could see his chiseled profile dark against the stars. He seemed to be listening to her aunt, but Kimberly was sure that what he really heard was the erratic patter of her own heart.

But he ignored Kimberly and spoke to Dodo, his voice satiny on the dark air. "Stories circulate," he said, "that valuable stones are hidden in the house—jewels even."

"Oh, that old tale." Dodo laughed almost girlishly. "Yes, it's even been said that the great topaz, the Heart of the Sun, is hidden somewhere among these stones. Such a rumor was inevitable. But the colonel always said that if anyone could find it here, they could *have* it. No, the topaz is long gone, I'm sure—Cyril Damon probably had it cut into a dozen smaller gems. He could live for the rest of his life on the price they'd bring. No, there's nothing to the old stories."

"A pity," Alec said smoothly. "Such a stone would fetch a fair price today. You could live like a princess again."

"Such a stone is beyond price," Dodo murmured softly. "And the days of splendor are over. But I saw them, and they were more wonderful than I can tell."

Kimberly felt tiny needles of discomfort piercing her. She was reminded of what Calvin had said, of how interested Alec had been in tales of her family and the colonel.

She tried to pull her awareness away from Alec's drugging nearness. What had Calvin called him—the young devil? That was Alec Shaughnessy, all right, a tall, lean, blue-eyed Prince of Darkness. And she, for one, had had enough of handsome devils who specialized in temptation.

She turned to him, tilting her head defiantly. "You should know better than to believe such stories, Mr. Shaughnessy. Or to try to dig them up."

There, she thought with satisfaction. That would teach him to pry into family business and collect rumors. His answer, however, caught her off balance.

"My profession is digging up such stories, my girl. You'd be surprised how common such legends are—I can name half a dozen houses in Australia with nearly identical rumors. I collect the stories, but I know the treasure story for what it is—a fiction. As far as I'm concerned, the most uncommon thing about this house is the warmth and courtesy of its hostess, your good aunt."

He raised his drink to Dodo in salute, then finished his sherry. He handed the empty glass to Kimberly. "Why don't you collect these glasses and wash them up. Help your aunt," he suggested smugly. "There's a good girl."

Kimberly's face burned, and she was grateful for the darkness. He had rebuked her neatly and put her in her place. She felt humiliated, like a child who has been reprimanded in front of visitors.

"Here, dear," said Lela Munroe smugly. "Just fill mine up again before you go."

Kimberly stood quickly and filled Lela's glass again. She began gathering up the other things with a vengeance.

"Oh, Kimberly," Dodo objected, "I'll do that—and I must turn down the beds."

"I'll turn down the beds," Kimberly answered, almost sharply. "You've worked hard all day. I'll wash the glasses, too. Sit, please, Aunt Dodo. You're tired, and I've got energy to burn."

She put her hand on Dodo's shoulder to keep her seated. Her aunt patted her hand fondly. "It's such a help having Kimberly home," she said, gazing up at her niece. "She's such a good-hearted child."

"She is a nice child," Alec Shaughnessy agreed pleasantly. "I'm sure she'll eventually turn out very well."

Devil, thought Kimberly angrily and wheeled away with the tray. She marched into the safety of the house and tried to take out her frustration by scalding the sherry glasses.

Everything was going wrong in her life, she thought darkly, running up the steep stairs. She had gone to Kansas City thinking she had enough talent to survive, then prosper and shine. She had been wrong.

The one man who'd interested her, Roger, had turned out to be married and a liar. Now she was home again, except it wasn't really home anymore, and her house was full of strangers on whom her aunt had to wait hand and foot.

She went into Lela Munroe's room, the one next to her own, and turned down the patchwork cotton quilt and freshly starched sheet.

She plumped the pillow, and, gritting her teeth, set a foil-wrapped mint on it. Dodo had read that all better hotels turned down guests' beds and left a complimentary treat on the pillow.

Kimberly didn't understand why grown people should be rewarded with candy for such a basic act as climbing into bed. But once Dodo got it into her head that something was proper, nothing could shake her out of her conviction. And Dodo really was starting to look frail, Kimberly thought unhappily. All her life she had given her efforts to others, and she deserved better than this servitude in her own home.

Alec Shaughnessy, Kimberly feared, as she entered his room, was going to be the last, maddening straw. Every time she saw him, he set her pulses galloping off. She did not want to react to him that way—she didn't want to react to any man ever again. She was still in shameful mourning for the disaster with Roger.

Alec confused and angered her. She thought she had come home because her heart was permanently broken, and Alec made her doubt that important truth. Worse, he seemed both to flirt with her and not flirt with her, to look at her as if she was a woman but talk to her and about her as if she were a child.

She turned back his covers almost savagely. She plumped his pillow by slapping the daylights out of it. She reached into the pocket of her pink sundress and took out the gold-wrapped mint. She set it on the starched pillow case as rebelliously as if it were tribute to a hated monarch.

"Steady," said Alec's mocking voice. "It's only a mint, you know. Didn't we talk this morning about your storms? You're fairly shooting lightning bolts."

Startled, she whirled. He stood in the doorway, tall and smiling wryly. The lamplight shone on the dark gold in his hair. He stepped into the room, gave her a knowing look and shut the door behind him.

She inched backward involuntarily. "Why," she demanded uneasily, "do you always creep up on me like that?"

"I don't creep," he murmured. "You're too busy listening to your own tumultuous thoughts to hear anything else. You turn down a bed nicely, by the way. Very nicely."

He took another step toward her, and Kimberly could move no farther away. She was against the double bed now. The big oak door, closed behind him, seemed suddenly ominous. "What are you doing here?" she breathed, looking up at him warily.

"This is my room," he explained with amused logic. "Do you mind? I've got work to do."

"Of course not." She looked in confusion at the old oak desk in the corner. It was cluttered with books, papers, a tape recorder and cassettes.

Then he was before her, looming over her. Her eyes swept back to him in confusion. She made the mistake of looking into his. They were blue and intensely serious, as startling and mesmerizing as always.

"Part of my work," he murmured, "seems cut out for me."

His hand moved to her upper arm, settling there authoritatively. "Come here, Kimberly. I'm going to teach you one of life's most important lessons."

She stared at him helplessly. His eyes were languorous now, full of heat and lazy desire.

"Don't," she warned him weakly. She snatched up the pillow and tried to clutch it to her as if it were a shield. The mint went skittering onto the carpet. "Stop—I know all about men like you—"

He took the pillow from her and threw it back on the bed. He put both hands on her arms. His touch made her feel at first shivery cold, then hot.

"You know nothing about men like me," he answered. Then he drew her closer, imprisoning her in the hard fortress of his arms.

His lips took hers, and her heart seemed to fly out through the open window into the starry night. Just as superstition had predicted, Kimberly was kissing a stranger.

CHAPTER THREE

KISSING ALEC, she thought giddily, was like dancing to some enchanted music. His lips commandeered hers, teaching them a vital and secret rhythm. Her blood, dizzied, drummed in her ears.

At first he kissed her with a deliberate and overpowering intensity. Just when she thought he had led her to the edge of some frightening sensual precipice, his mouth grew gentle against her own.

Her lips tingled, his languid assault wreaking as much tumult on her senses as his more forceful one. That slow, haunting kiss seemed to tell her that he could sweetly torment her like this all night long.

Then just as she was yielding, melting into that quiet melody of touch and taste, his mouth became passionate again against her own. She felt a longing so sharp it burnt through her like fire. He twined his fingers in the long brown silk of her hair, while his lips continued to teach her all the perilous meanings of yearning.

She was in danger of being swept away, when his kisses became light, taunting, almost playful. For the first time she noticed that his mustache tickled. Momentarily she gave herself up to that sensation. There were, she thought in pleased bewilderment, more ways to make love than she could have ever imagined.

Alec led her down first one path of desire, then another, then another still. He lured her first this way, then that. She could not get her breath. She gave a sob that was half protest, half plea for him to show her more of the secrets that he knew.

Instead he drew back. Through hooded eyes he studied her rosy, swollen lips. He slid one of the dress's pink straps down, then pressed hot, moist lips against her bare shoulder.

"Don't—" she almost begged. "Don't kiss me anyplace else—please—" She turned her face up to his again, waiting the wedding of his lips to hers.

Instead he cupped his fingers around her chin and stared down into her dazed dark eyes. "You see?" he asserted softly. "You thought you'd never kiss again. But you have, and nicely, too. You thought your heart would never beat so swiftly again, but it does—I feel it."

What he said was true. She knew he must feel her heart hammering against the hardness of his chest. And she could feel the pounding of his, strong and steady, against her breasts.

Biting her lip, she forced herself back to reality. She went extremely still in his arms. "Stop," she said, her voice going cold. "Let go of me."

He lightly kissed her sun-browned shoulder again. "I'm only showing you—you thought you'd never feel desire again. You're not a shattered woman. You're warm and whole. And even willing, if you'd admit it."

He dipped his head and placed a hot, exploratory kiss just above the velvety valley between her breasts. Kimberly gasped. She was unsure which was worse: his arrogance or her unhappy realization that his arrogance might be fully justified. She had been warm and willing, all right. She must also have been mad.

She struggled away from him, but without complete success. He grasped her by the arms to keep her from slipping away completely. "What's the matter?" he drawled insolently. "Does the truth scare you? Your heart wasn't broken in Kansas City. Only your pride was hurt."

She tossed her head rebelliously. "I never would have let you kiss me—except I'm—I'm rebounding from someone else. I loved him. I knew I had to kiss somebody else someday. It might as well be you. I don't feel anything for you. What happened between you and me was just—nothing. Meaningless."

"What happened between us was hardly nothing. It has to do with basic biology. Sex, if you will. And the difference between love and sex," he said dryly, "is mostly imaginary. Men and women don't fall in love. They either fall into bed—or they don't. Your problem is simply that you're so deliciously ripe, so perfectly ripe. And ready to fall."

"Don't delude yourself," Kimberly retorted, eyes snapping in resentment. It would be too humiliating if what he said were true. "If I went to bed with anybody, it wouldn't be with a conceited Casanova like you. The whole female population of Australia probably took up a collection to send you overseas. Who do you think you are? God's gift to women?"

She pulled away from his grasp, breathing hard, and pushed up the strap of her dress. She tossed her long hair out of her eyes.

"There's this to be said for Casanova," Alec said, smiling crookedly at her anger. "He did what he did very well. But you don't want to think about it, do you? Well, get back to me when you do. It's going to be a long, hot summer." He opened the door for her, mockery shining from his eyes. "Good night, Kimberly."

"Long, hot summer or not, it'll be a cold day in hell before I ever—" she began through gritted teeth.

He put his finger to her lips, silencing her. He ushered her toward the open door. Then he lay his finger on the tip of her nose. "Yes, yes, a cold day in hell, the moon will be blue, et cetera, et cetera. But one of these nights hell may chill and the moon may turn blue. As I said, good night."

He closed the door after her. Almost immediately the smile fell from his face. The air in the room still seemed to radiate sexual tension. Alec frowned and shook his head.

He had meant only to initiate a flirtation to divert her. Something more had happened. Touching the girl had set something off in him he had not expected. He would have to be more careful. Far more careful. He shook his head.

Kimberly, having been ejected into the hall, looked at the closed door in confusion and mounting rage.

What happened? she thought, stunned. He had just insulted her in almost every way possible. She was so furious she felt faint. Fighting the feeling, she turned and kicked the door as hard as she could. The sound echoed throughout the house, reverberating on the night.

She stalked downstairs and out into the garden. After a moment Dodo stood at the back door, peering out into the darkness. "Kimberly?" she said hesitantly. "I heard the most dreadful noise."

"It was nothing," Kimberly said, inhaling deeply and staring up at the stars. The fragrance of the roses made her half giddy. "I saw a—a cockroach."

"A cockroach!" Dodo said in horror. "Oh, mercy! Don't tell anyone. There has never been a cockroach in this house—never!"

"Yes," Kimberly said darkly. She squared her shoulders. "Well, somehow one got in." Above her, the stars seemed to spin drunkenly. The silver of the moon looked pale blue.

What's happening to me? she thought. *What's happening?*

THE NEXT MORNING she decided the best thing would be not to show an iota of emotion. With enormous false calm she set the china plate of hot biscuits down on the table between Lela Munroe and Alec Shaughnessy. Lela was resplendent in a lacy white pantsuit, her flyaway hair ornamented with barrettes of pearl and rhinestone.

"Good morning, Miss Simpson-Dodge," Alec murmured with maddening cheer. "And how is your poor foot?"

Kimberly gave him a look so cold that his mustache should have frosted.

"Foot?" asked Dodo in confusion, pouring Lela Munroe's coffee. "Foot?"

Alec smiled his slow half smile. He wore a blue shirt, which should have been against the law, because it made his eyes look almost supernaturally blue and his skin more bronzed than ever. "The bang in the hall last night. Your niece tripped herself up. Be careful, Miss Simpson-Dodge. Who knows into what dangerous place you might fall."

"I didn't trip," Kimberly said icily. She recalled his accusation that she was ripe and yearning to fall into someone's bed, preferably his. "And I don't intend to fall anywhere." She took her own place at the table.

Lela Munroe, slathering butter on a steaming biscuit, shot Kimberly a measuring look. "Why," she demanded, "is your name Simpson-Dodge? Was your mother one of these liberated women who wouldn't give up her own name and insisted on being hyphenated? An uppity system, in my opinion. One last name ought to be enough for anyone. Especially a little sprout like you."

Dodo looked slightly stricken, and Alec Shaughnessy glanced at Kimberly with one eyebrow cocked.

"My grandfather, the colonel, didn't approve of my mother's marriage," Kimberly said evenly. "He was right.

It didn't work. When she came home, he insisted she give up her married name. They compromised in my case.''

"I see," Lela Munroe said snidely. "So people knew you actually did have a father. Legally, that is.''

"Oh, he was completely legal," Kimberly replied. She was beginning to dislike Lela Munroe almost as much as she did Alec Shaughnessy. "He just wasn't much good. He thought he was a ladies' man—you know the type. I say whoever wants that sort is welcome to them.'' She smiled sweetly at both Lela and Alec, then gave her attention to unfolding her napkin.

"Oh," came Dodo's fluttery voice, her large eyes wounded, "it's just that my sister was very...sheltered. She was not the best judge of character.''

"She was also desperate," Kimberly muttered brazenly. She no longer cared what Lela Munroe thought of her. "I suppose she thought it was her last chance. Falling for a womanizer like my father is about as desperate as you can get. There's a story that in our family women are best off avoiding men.'' She gave Alec a disdainful glance. "So far it's proven true.''

Alec looked at her over the rim of his coffee cup. "But some good came of the marriage, Miss Simpson-Dodge,'' he said smoothly. "You. And as for avoiding men, that, as you say, is only a story. Surely you wouldn't let a mere fairy tale govern your life.''

"I try to let sense govern my life," Kimberly retorted. But in spite of her brave words, she hadn't done a very good job of it, she thought glumly. Still, she kept her chin held high.

Dodo, clearly nervous at the turn the conversation had taken, tried to change the subject. "My," she said, holding out her coffee cup. "Look how trembly I am this morning. It must be because I didn't sleep well last night. I could have sworn I heard someone in the attic.''

"Someone in the attic?" Lela Munroe asked in mild alarm.

"Probably squirrels," Kimberly said. "I'll check on it today."

"White squirrels?" asked Alec Shaughnessy with a derisive smile. "Bringing change to the household?"

"Squirrels," sniffed Lela, "can be rabid. You can't be too careful."

"Quite right," Alec said, nodding at her sagacity. "Perhaps I should check the attic. Stalking the savage squirrel is no job for a lady."

"Oh, really, I couldn't allow it," Dodo objected. "You're our *guest*, Mr. Shaughnessy. It's not right."

"I insist," he said. "I could hardly think of myself as a gentleman otherwise. Please allow me."

Kimberly darted him a sarcastic glance at the word *gentleman*. He smiled at her. The gleam in his eye was not gentlemanly at all.

LELA MUNROE set off for Spring Street to inflict major damage on her credit cards. Alec Shaughnessy informed Dodo that he had a morning appointment with a local farmer to talk about superstitions concerning animals, but that he would return by noon to inspect the attic for the marauding squirrels.

"Such a nice man," Dodo murmured, watching him set off in his rented Thunderbird convertible. "So considerate. So gentlemanly. We must give him lunch."

"In that case, I won't be hungry," Kimberly muttered. She left her aunt looking puzzled and went upstairs to make up the guests' rooms. Mrs. Munroe's was as untidy as possible. Expensive clothes were strewn everywhere, including the floor. Kimberly picked them up, put them back on hangers and hung them in the closet.

One of Dodo's excesses was changing sheets every day. Kimberly stripped the bed and put on freshly starched sheets. She was sure Dodo was killing herself with all this fuss.

Her face flushed with anger and embarrassment when she approached Alec's door. She remembered last night's scene with chagrin. She had responded all too eagerly to his touch. Even if he was right, and her heart wasn't broken, what did he think? That she was eager for a meaningless affair? He had another think coming, she fumed.

She turned the knob of his door and was surprised when it didn't move. She tried again. It was locked. She stared at it, disturbed. If he didn't want his room made up, why hadn't he simply said so at breakfast?

She stared at the door in perturbation for a moment. Perhaps he'd locked it accidentally. But maybe he hadn't. She remembered nervously the legend of Bluebeard and his forbidden locked room. Curious women could never resist looking inside, and the temptation, alas, was always disastrous.

Nonsense, Kimberly thought. She was being dramatic again. She set the fresh sheets on the hall table and ran downstairs to get the key ring. Nevertheless she was careful to say nothing about the locked room to Dodo. Her aunt, she was sure, would be horrified if she even imagined a guest's privacy was being violated.

Glancing nervously about, Kimberly unlocked the door and swung it open. Morning sun poured through the windows, making the white curtains glow. The room was neat as a pin, the bed already made.

She frowned, looking about. The books and papers that had been scattered so haphazardly on the desk the night before were nowhere in evidence. She looked in the closet. The books were there, stacked on the highest shelf. She brought over the desk chair and stood on it, peering at their titles.

Nothing suspicious, she thought, feeling almost disappointed. They were all folklore books on Australia, New Zealand, the United States, Canada. She sighed, got off the chair and returned it to its place.

Try as she might, she was unable to resist opening each of the desk drawers and peering in. The first contained a collection of folders. Attached to the top one was a sheaf of notes in a bold blue scribble. "How to tell a virgin," said one. "Slight indentation in tip of nose; disappears when virginity is taken. Reflection in mirror not as bright for experienced woman: mirror loses 'shine' when girl loses virginity."

She blushed and stuffed the folder back into the drawer. Her eyes were drawn to her reflection in the mirror of the antique dresser. She was drenched in sunshine from the window, and her reflection fairly shone.

"Idiotic superstitions," she thought, opening the last drawer in an idle gesture. What kind of job was this for a grown man anyway, running all over the world collecting stupid stories?

The bottom drawer slid open. She blinked in surprise. It contained a box of Indian design. It looked almost familiar, yet she was sure her grandfather had never owned such a box. On its lid, in a mosaic of mother-of-pearl, was the Hindu god Ganesha.

As a child, looking through her grandfather's treasures, Kimberly had always been most taken by the images of Ganesha. Chubby, kindly looking, with a large belly and an elephant's head, Ganesha was the deity of good fortune and overcoming obstacles. One by one her grandfather had sold the family treasures, gifts from the rajah. The last to go had been the small silver statue of Ganesha on his throne.

She touched the box with admiring fingers. How odd, she thought, for Alec Shaughnessy to have such an object. He had never expressed any special interest in India other than his polite attention to Dodo's stories.

That, she thought, gnawing on her lower lip, and his questioning of Calvin about her family. She took the box from the drawer and tried to open it. It was locked. She shook it slightly. Within it, weight shifted. It was not empty. It sounded as if it contained papers. She stared at it in frustration, then placed it carefully back in the drawer.

She picked up the sheets from the dresser and held them in her arms, staring at his bed, its patchwork cover, so merry and innocent looking in the morning light. She decided against making his bed over. He didn't need to know she had been in his room. She would leave the sheets on the hall table and ask him outright why he had locked his door.

But as she stepped toward the hall, she crossed the spot where, last night, he had held her in his arms and kissed her with such intimacy and such knowledge. Her stomach did an odd little dance within her. Recalling his touch, the feel of his mouth upon her own, made her mind spin, her knees go a bit weak.

Quickly she left the room, locking it once more, as if she could lock her emotions and memories up safely inside, imprisoning them. But she could not. They followed her down the hall and then down the stairs and haunted her all morning long.

When Alec Shaughnessy returned to the house precisely at noon, as he'd promised, Kimberly asked him tersely why he'd locked his door. He smiled benignly and said he was capable of picking up after himself and that Dodo worked too hard.

Dodo insisted he have lunch with them, and at last he acquiesced. Kimberly, keeping aloof, said she wasn't hungry.

Then she went off, her temper and her stomach both growling, to do the laundry so Dodo wouldn't have to.

She tried to ignore Alec when he descended, dusty and streaked with sweat, after two hours in the attic. He had searched the north half thoroughly, he said, and found a hole near the eaves where a squirrel might get through, and yes, it did look as if animals might have been playing in the attic.

Dodo's beautiful eyes looked distracted by this new trouble, but Alec soothed her, saying he would inspect the rest of the attic tomorrow and patch any holes he found. He mustn't go to such trouble, Dodo fussed. It was no trouble, he said, to help a lady like Dodo.

Kimberly, who had been helping her aunt tally up the household accounts, slipped Alec a look of ill-disguised disgust. He would have kissed Dodo's hand if he thought he could have gotten away with it, she thought murderously, the odious flatterer.

He ignored her hostility and turned to her, smiling down. "One thing you might do for me, Miss Simpson-Dodge, is bring me some extra towels. I'm going to have to shower."

"Oh, dear, oh, dear," Dodo said, staring in horror at his blue shirt with its patches of sweat and dirt. "I really should dust the attic—it's a scandal. One does tend to let an attic go."

"Nobody dusts an attic," Kimberly protested, "Really, Dodo, be realistic."

Dodo looked wounded. Alec Shaughnessy patted the older woman's small hand.

"Some towels, Miss Simpson-Dodge? If you don't mind?" he said to Kimberly, arching one dark brow. His mouth curved in a sarcastic smile.

Kimberly marched off to fetch fresh towels, swearing under her breath. Dodo probably would take it into her head to mop and wax the attic. Of course Kimberly couldn't allow her to do it and would end up doing the chore herself, all because Alec Shaughnessy had gotten his precious body smirched with vile dust. She stamped into the laundry room and got warm towels from the drier.

Two at a time, she ran up the stairs then felt her heart sink when she reached the second floor. Alec's door was ajar. He was inside. He had her grandfather's old room, the only one with a private bath. She didn't want to enter the room again with him in it. She rapped at the door with more confidence than she felt.

He swung it open lazily and stood there, shirtless, his sun-gilded torso shining with perspiration. "Yes?" he said, giving her a bored glance. "The towels? You may hang them up. There's a good girl."

She squeezed past him, darting toward the bathroom, but not before his image seemed to have burned itself permanently into her mind. His shoulders were wide, his chest hard and muscular, hazed with curling dark hair. His stomach was flat, his waist narrow as it tapered to his flat hips in their faded jeans. One lock of bronzed hair fell over his eyes, and he stood with his hands easily on his hips.

Shaken by the perfection of his half nakedness, she hung up the fluffy towels and scolded herself for even noticing him. *"The towels? You may hang them up. There's a good girl."* She mentally mocked his superior tone. She hoped he slipped in the shower and landed on his classic nose.

She inched her way out of the bathroom and edged by him. He hadn't moved an inch. He still stood, his hands on his hips, the same half smile on his lips. "Thank you very much, Miss Simpson-Dodge," he said, smirking down at her.

She shot him an icy glance. "Stop calling me Miss Simpson-Dodge," she ordered. "I don't like it."

"Want to stay and scrub my back?" he invited in his huskiest voice. "Kimberly?"

She slammed the door with a force that shook the wall. She flounced downstairs.

"What on earth was *that* noise?" Dodo asked, her hands quivering in horror around her face.

"I saw that cockroach again," Kimberly prevaricated, her face burning.

"Oh, dear, oh, dear, oh, dear," Dodo said tragically. "Rampaging squirrels *and* a cockroach—whatever will we do?"

Kimberly was silent, not knowing in the slightest what was to be done.

Upstairs, Alec Shaughnessy walked to the window and leaned the heels of both hands on the sill. He stared moodily down into that improbable garden suspended over the mountain's side.

The afternoon sunshine played across his bronzed features. He'd managed to keep smiling, to stay playful while the girl was around, but he wasn't smiling now. Consternation and conflict shone in his blue eyes. *What's happening here?* he wondered.

What indeed? the house around him seemed to mock.

KIMBERLY SPENT the afternoon working in the garden. Weeds were springing rampantly in the fertile warmth of May. The roses needed pruning badly, and the borders of phlox had gone ragged over the years. It seemed that every hour she spent in the house, she noticed more things that needed fixing. She was still on her hands and knees at suppertime, when Dodo called her in.

Dodo said mournfully that the kitchen plumbing was moaning and groaning again. "This house!" Kimberly exclaimed, rolling her eyes heavenward. "Why don't we just sell it before it runs us both into the ground?"

Dodo turned her great, innocent eyes reproachfully on her niece. "Why, Kimberly," she breathed, in true shock. "I promised the colonel I never would sell. And I never will. Ever. And you mustn't, either. Those were his wishes."

What about our wishes? Kimberly thought rebelliously. If they sold the house, there would be enough for Dodo to live modestly for the rest of her life in a smaller, more sensible dwelling. Kimberly could escape somewhere, anywhere—go off to art school perhaps or just stay in Eureka and start a shop, anything but spend her life in bondage to this house.

She picked at her salad. She didn't see how Dodo had done it alone, and she didn't see, frankly, how the two of them were going to do it together. The garden was symbolic of the whole place—going to weed and seed and slow ruin.

"We need help," Kimberly said firmly. "Especially in the garden. We could use a handyman. There are squirrels in the attic and spooks in the kitchen pipes. The window in my room is jammed again, and the basement steps need fixing."

"We can't afford help," Dodo said.

"Well," Kimberly answered, rubbing her aching back, "we've got to find it somehow."

Dodo chose to ignore her as delicately as possible. They heard the front door swing open. "Oh, that must be Mr. Shaughnessy," she said happily. "I must set up the sherry tray. I've made some little cakes, too."

"You treat these guests like royalty," Kimberly grumbled.

"Oh," Dodo said, her face filling with light, "but that's how they should be treated—I remember how wonderful it felt to be pampered in India. And I don't mind—the house seems so full of life with everyone here."

Kimberly looked at her aunt's faded but still-lovely face. She felt a lump in her throat. Suddenly she understood what was keeping Dodo going, despite all the hard work and adversity. For the first time in her adult life, Dodo felt she was living. The guests in the house were not mere temporary tenants to her, they were truly cherished guests—the people she had wanted in her life for years. After decades of being the colonel's devoted slave, Dodo was lonely no more.

Kimberly swallowed back any criticism she might make. She watched, her throat still choked, as Dodo cleared the kitchen table and flew about the room, arranging the sherry tray and her cakes. But she refused to join her aunt and the guests on the porch. Her emotions were too tangled.

She stayed in the living room, curled up on the old rose-colored velvet love seat. Across from her the massive fireplace that the colonel had built dominated the large room. Made of great chunks of colored quartz, it twinkled in the muted light from the reading lamp.

Even Dodo knew better than to explain to guests about the beautiful enameled Indian vase that sat on a natural shelf formed by one of the darker crystals. The copper vase, lidded and ornamented with designs of dancing Hindu maidens, contained the colonel's ashes. It was his express wish that his remains be placed there, as if he wished to dominate that house even from the afterlife.

Kimberly had quickly taught herself to ignore the presence of the vase. As far as she was concerned, it wasn't there. She had her sketch book open and was trying to draw a white squirrel, but her fingers were cramped and disobedient from pulling weeds all afternoon. She heard the voices drifting from the front porch: Mrs. Munroe's, strident and self-important, then Alec Shaughnessy's, low and mocking and Dodo's, reverent and soft as she talked about the colonel and India.

"At night," Dodo was saying, "the summer palace was covered with tens of thousands of tiny lights, as if all the fireflies in the world had gathered there. And in the daytime, peacocks walked in the courtyard, and the fountain ran with perfumed waters. Every dawn and dusk the Maharaja's band saluted the journey of the sun. Their uniforms were blue and silver, and their turbans white as snow, and their instruments were ornamented with the purest gold . . . and my sister and I were treated like princesses."

Kimberly cast down her sketch book. All her work looked hopelessly mediocre to her. She went out the back door to sit in the garden. The air was warm and oppressively still. Lightning played in the distant mountains, forking down in silent flashes that briefly lit the peaks.

She sat on the wrought iron seat, leaning her head back wearily against the rough bark of the catalpa tree. The heavy fragrance of the roses was like an opiate. Bone-tired, she slipped into an uneasy drowse, dreaming of roses and peacocks and scented fountains and a man with a dangerous smile.

Then she was awake again. The air was no longer warm, but chill, and the night was no longer silent. The sky was perfectly black, and wind keened eerily among the trees, making the roses rustle and bend.

"So there you are," said Alec Shaughnessy, standing over her.

She blinked up in surprise. He was like a figure made entirely of shadows. She shuddered back to awareness, suddenly conscious of the night's coolness and the coming storm.

He extended his hands and drew her to her feet. She was too disoriented to object. "Nobody knew where you'd gone," Alec breathed, still holding her hands. "Your aunt thought perhaps you'd slipped off to town to listen to music or meet friends."

The wind rose higher. Feeling slightly otherworldly, for once Kimberly didn't bother to resist Alec. His hands, so warm and strong around hers, seemed the only real things in a dark and bewitched world. "I don't have that many friends," she said softly. "My grandfather—the colonel— liked us to keep to ourselves."

"Kept you prisoner in his castle, did he? Perhaps I don't blame him. If you were mine, I might keep you locked away for myself, too—and let the rest of the world go to blazes."

He raised her hands so that they were pressed against the hardness of his chest. He held them there. Lightning flickered, closer now, and for a moment his handsome face glimmered silver in its inconstant glow. In that brief span, she saw how intent his expression was, how seriously he stared down at her.

Her heart began to hammer, to run as wild as the wind that tossed and gusted.

"You don't want to trust me, do you?" he asked, his voice both harsh and gentle at the same time.

In the distance, thunder murmured like a warning. "No," she answered, looking up at his shadowy features. "I don't. I can't."

"Then perhaps you're a wise girl, Kimberly," he said huskily. "Or perhaps we're both fools. Because whether we like it or not, something seems to be occurring between us."

Once more the lightning darted whitely, and Kimberly felt as if it had struck her through the heart. "Occurring?" she breathed. It seemed an odd word, far too formal to describe what she was feeling.

His hands moved to her arms. He nodded. He said nothing more, but his touch was warm and dizzying.

"No," Kimberly protested softly. "Nothing's ... occurring."

"Wrong," Alec said tautly. "You may pretend your heart is broken. I may pretend that you merely amuse me. But something stronger than pretence has us in its grasp. A sort of madness in the blood. You can feel it. So can I."

"No," Kimberly repeated, but she felt hypnotized, unable to break away. The roses danced in the dark wind.

He drew her to him with a movement swifter than the lightning's. He bent over her, his arms going round her tightly. "Your mind doesn't trust me, love," he whispered, his warm breath fanning her cheek. "But your body does. The body has its own wisdom. Listen to it."

The wind gusted coolly, tossing her hair, whipping the skirt of her yellow dress. His arms seemed warm and safe, yet she knew that with him safety was an illusion. "I have to go in," she repeated, trying to fight the mesmerizing power his body held over hers. "Dodo needs me."

"No," he said almost fiercely, for the wind threatened to carry his words away. "Her day is over. She's turned down the covers and laid out her chocolates and, like a child, babbled herself half to sleep with tales of happier times in India."

Kimberly's myriad worries came tumbling back into her mind. "Why do you encourage her to go on and on like that about India?" she asked, her voice trembling. "It's not good for her. I don't want her living in the past—"

"I do it because I'm fond of her, and my listening makes her happy," he said with the same intensity. "Ask me a better question—such as why I don't throttle you for sneaking into my room when the door is locked and pawing through my things.''

The lightning shimmered again. Momentarily she could see his face. He was smiling, but his smile was cold. She was suddenly profoundly uneasy. ''I wanted to know why you'd locked the door,'' she said, pushing away from him, but he held her fast.

''And what did you find, my curious little cat?'' he asked. ''Anything to pique your melodramatic imagination?''

''I didn't find anything,'' she retorted. ''How did you know I was there?''

She had stopped trying to escape from him. He held her too firmly. ''I have my ways,'' he said vaguely. ''And what did you think you'd find?''

His arms tightened round her. His face bent closer.

Kimberly gasped, half in pain and half in anticipation. ''I don't know.''

The wind rose again, wailing and making her shiver. The flowers danced madly in the gusts. ''You're a maddening creature,'' he accused. ''You've ransacked my room, you've stalked about all day ignoring me, and now you're trembling in my arms as if you could never be held closely enough.''

''I'm trembling because I'm cold,'' she lied, biting her lower lip.

''No,'' he breathed harshly. ''You're not cold, Kimberly. You're anything but cold.''

''I have to go in,'' she said for the third time. ''My aunt needs me.''

''No,'' he stated between gritted teeth. ''I need you.''

His lips bore down hers, and Kimberly felt as if she were being carried into the heart of the stormy darkness.

The lightning gleamed briefly on them. Neither of them felt the first drops of rain pelt icily down on them, or the wind whip even more wildly. They had traveled to where no weather exists except the weather of desire.

CHAPTER FOUR

IT WAS ALEC who at last drew away, his breathing uneven. In the windswept darkness, Kimberly felt the rain falling like cold jewels on her hair, her face, her clothing.

Alec's arms around her were warm, and the night smelled of roses and summer storm. He put his hand beneath the long, blowing veil of her hair, his fingers cradling the back of her neck. The wind blew long strands of her hair across her lips, and he kissed them anyway, then drew back once more.

"I think I could die for you," he said harshly. "Die with wanting you. How did this happen, Kimberly? I never meant to want you. I never planned on wanting anyone. Not like this. And not you. Of all people."

The lightning glared, lighting the sky with its cold blue-white flare. Almost simultaneously the thunder blasted. Kimberly shivered and Alec held her more tightly, protecting her from the lashing of the wind.

"You," he repeated, his voice ragged. "Of all people. I don't think that's thunder, my love. It's the gods, laughing their heads off."

"What do you mean?" she asked breathlessly. The rain on her eyelashes blurred his shadowy image even further.

He released her but kept his body close to hers. He used both hands to smooth back her hair and frame her face.

"Nothing, love," he muttered, kissing her, but this time holding his passion in check. "Only that I mustn't find you out here only to let you drown." He kissed her again, with even greater restraint. "Into the house with you. I'll follow in a moment."

"I..." murmured Kimberly, but could say nothing more.

"This is so fast it dizzies even me," he warned. "Leave me, Kimberly, while I can still let you go. The situation wants cool heads and the light of day."

His hands fell away from her face. He took a step backward, his arms slightly outstretched from his sides as in a gesture of release. Lightning flickered again, this time farther away, dancing in the distant mountains.

Kimberly stood, her long hair flowing like a mermaid's in the rain and the wind. Her wet dress clung to her thighs and swathed her in coldness.

"Go," he repeated, as the darkness fell again. "If you still want me in the light of day—we'll see then."

Confused and suddenly chilled to the marrow, she stared at his tall form, indistinct in the stormy night. What did he mean with all this talk of wanting? Of the light of day? Of course, she wanted him....

Want, she thought in desperation. *Not love, just want.* Pure and meaningless, like the animals. Not even as much feeling as Roger had shown for her.

She took a deep breath, her thoughts darting as wildly as the fugitive leaves in the wind. Desire—was that all he felt? She felt more for him, she was certain. Yet how could she? It was impossible. And all he spoke of was physical longing, a common urge.

"Go," he ordered again.

She turned and fled, whether from him or from what he'd awakened in her, she didn't know. He stood in the driving rain, watching her disappear into the house, where a light still shone.

He stepped away from the creaking limbs of the catalpa tree and stood in the open, looking after her. The rain pasted his shirt against his chest, tossed his hair across his brow. He clenched his left fist and then held it in his right hand so tightly that his knuckles cracked.

The wind stabbed through him like an icy blade. What had come over him? He had meant only for her to be briefly infatuated with him, nothing more. He had meant to feel nothing, himself. He couldn't afford to feel anything. Yet there, in the rain and the roses, he had felt far too much.

He was a man who planned everything, but things were happening that he could not have foreseen. How could he have known that desire for this woman would blaze through him with such intensity? What she awoke in him was as powerful as it was unexpected. He—so fond of certainties—didn't know precisely what would happen next.

He shook the rain from his eyes. What happened next, he supposed, was up to her. It depended on whatever her fiery little spirit might feel in the cold light of day.

THE MORNING LIGHT fell across Kimberly's closed eyes. Drowsily, as if troubled by her dreams, she tried to wipe the sunshine away. Then her eyes fluttered opened. It was not a dream that had made her sleep so uneasily. It was reality.

She sat up with a start. She wore a pair of sand-brown pajamas, cut like a boy's, and her long hair was plaited into two braids and pinned atop her head like a crown. She looked across the room into her bureau mirror and saw a dark-eyed girl whose bare face looked no more than fifteen years old. She sat, surrounded by the innocent glow of early sunlight.

Her face flushed, growing hot. She jumped from her bed and made it up with smooth precision, patting every wrinkle out of place. But her thoughts were anything but precise. If guilt put wrinkles on the soul, all the patting and straightening in the world wouldn't have smoothed hers away.

Images of the night before tumbled back in humiliating confusion. She remembered clinging to Alec in the dark torrents of the storm and wanting to cling to him forever. She blushed harder, thinking of that.

She remembered the dizzying sensation of his arms crushing her close and his mouth bearing down upon her own. Once again she heard him telling her to go while he could still let her go, and she recalled all too well that she had not wanted to leave him.

She stole another furtive glance at herself in the mirror. Surely such wantonness should show on a woman, she thought shamefully. It did not. A brown-eyed tomboy seemed to be looking back, no worse for erotic wear.

She shook her head. In mortification she recalled how she'd fled inside and torn off the wet clothes that he had touched as if they offended her conscience. Beneath the stinging spray of the hot shower, she'd tried to scrub all memory of him away and scald herself clean.

She'd donned her most modest pajamas, braided her wet hair and put it up primly, then climbed into bed as demurely as a virgin must climb back onto a lonely altar, her virtue still intact—although barely.

Now she shed the pajamas and put on her clothing quickly, as if she didn't want to pay too much attention to a body that had already come too close to betraying her. The shorts she picked were pale blue and stylishly baggy. The matching oversized T-shirt she put on was large enough for several Kimberlies and all their modesty as well.

Good grief, she thought, brushing out her hair. How could she have thought she wanted the man? Maybe he'd awakened her when she was dreaming of Roger, and somehow, in the darkness and the storm—no, she thought. That wasn't true. She hadn't thought of Roger once when she was in Alec's arms. In her present consternation, in fact, she had trouble picturing Roger's dark face.

She brushed so hard at her hair that her long tresses crackled with electricity. The braiding had made her hair wavy and full-bodied. The better, she thought, to hide the rest of her, for she did not want to face the day or herself or her disgraceful memories. Most of all, she didn't want to face Alec Shaughnessy.

What horrible thing had he said? That if she still wanted him by the light of day—well, then, what? He hadn't elaborated. It was just as well, because she didn't want him, wouldn't want him, couldn't want him. She had certainly cast off the brief and incredible illusion that she felt something akin to affection for him.

After all, she lectured herself, putting on the barest touch of lipstick, she could feel neither genuine affection nor desire for the man. Her heart was permanently broken over Roger Birch, artist and traitor. But for a broken heart, she noticed as she fastened her sandals, hers was beating incredibly hard.

She opened her door and peered nervously down the hall. He didn't seem to be up yet. The house itself had the air of dozing and peaceful dreaming in the early morning quiet. She tiptoed swiftly down the stairs.

She would make coffee and set the table, start some cinnamon rolls perhaps. But first, foremost, she must compose herself so that when she saw Alec she would register no emotion whatsoever. This, she told herself, should be easy.

But when she walked into the kitchen, he was there. His back to her, he was turning on the burner beneath the teakettle. He wore khaki slacks and a short-sleeved shirt striped with white and khaki. In the light that poured through the white kitchen curtains, his hair seemed somehow more shot through with gold than usual.

He turned. Kimberly's heart did some kind of soaring ballet leap within her chest, as his jewel-blue eyes met her dark ones. Beneath his mustache, his mouth curved in a slow smile.

"It's morning," he said. "Couldn't sleep actually. Hope you fared better."

"I fared just fine," Kimberly lied, looking up into his eyes.

Oh, no, she thought. As impossible as it was, she felt the same surge of sweet longing for him she'd felt the night before. It was still there, in the bright, untarnished light of day.

His eyes held hers. A silent dialogue seemed to course between them.

Do you feel the same?

Yes. Do you?

Yes.

What now? What next?

Yes. What now? What next?

"You look so solemn," he said at last, his smile one-sided and rueful. "I should have hoped you'd look happy. Aren't you happy?"

"Yes," she breathed. She supposed she was happy. Yet mixed with her unexpected joy was fear.

"You need a pale blue ribbon," he murmured, "to tie back your bonny brown hair and let your lovely face show. I'll buy you one."

He stretched his hand out to smooth her hair back from her cheek, but at that moment Dodo fluttered in, tying the sash of her lacy apron. Alec's hand fell back to his side. Somewhat too nonchalantly, he slid it into the pocket of his slacks. "Good day, Miss Simpson," he said, his cheerfulness only a shade too innocent.

"Oh," Kimberly said guiltily, moving toward the coffee maker, "Dodo. Good morning. I guess I'm up a little early."

"Are you?" Dodo asked worriedly. "I'm not late, am I? It wouldn't do at all for the hostess to oversleep—"

The shrilling of the teakettle interrupted her. "What? What's this? Oh, Mr. Shaughnessy! Making your own tea! We can't have this. Sit down, sit down. Or take a turn in the garden. I'll do this—it's my duty."

"I've made tea before, Miss Simpson," Alec smiled. He spoke to Dodo, but his eyes stayed on Kimberly. "Turning on a kettle won't do me in."

"Shoo!" Dodo ordered with surprising authority. "There I was, a slug-a-bed, with my poor guest making do for himself. Oh, I must have overslept—those squirrels kept me awake again, moving half the night in the attic."

Alec's smile vanished. "You heard them again?"

"Oh, dear, yes." Dodo bustled, measuring out the tea leaves. "I can hear a pin drop. My vision may be fuzzy, but my hearing is sharp. Oh, I heard it, all right."

"I'll have another look today," Alec assured her. "Patch that hole up. Did you hear anything, Miss Simpson-Dodge?" His smile, half-mocking, had returned.

"No. Nothing," Kimberly replied in confusion. She kept her attention focused on sorting out the proper silverware. The bright kitchen seemed alive with all sorts of emotions that only she and Alec could perceive. Dodo, intent now on the skillet, seemed oblivious to the lively undercurrents of feeling.

Alec drifted from the kitchen and strolled out to the garden, where a few drops of rain still glittered in the sun. He stopped near the catalpa tree and stared out at the mountains.

Kimberly watched him through the sheer white curtains. He stood on the exact spot where he'd held her in his arms the night before. Again her heart took that odd, almost painful leap. Why, she wondered, did he suddenly look so hard-faced, almost brooding?

Breakfast seemed an elaborate charade to Kimberly, with both she and Alec pretending not to take special notice of each other. But she was aware of the bolts of feeling and awareness that fairly danced in the air.

Dodo, concentrating mightily on all the properties of genteel breakfasting, didn't notice. Neither did Lela Munroe, resplendent this morning in shocking pink. Lela smiled girlishly at Alec all through the meal. The woman practically grinned, even with a mouthful of eggs, Kimberly thought unkindly.

"Why, I'm going to be downtown this morning, too," Lela told Alec coquettishly. "We might as well go together. We could meet for lunch, too—I'll show you this astonishing little hole-in-the-wall place I've discovered. They make the most scrumptious strudel."

"I'm sorely tempted," Alec replied with a forced smile. "But I've promised Miss Simpson to stalk her pillaging squirrel. It disturbs her sleep. We can't have that."

Lela looked down her nose at Dodo. "I thought it was Miss Simpson's duty to take care of us," she said sweetly, "not the other way around."

"One must do unto others," Alec said with pleasant piety.

"All the time?" Lela asked snidely and gave both Dodo and Kimberly a disagreeable glance. "Shouldn't you tie all that hair back, by the way, Miss Simpson-Dodge? I wouldn't want to be finding any of it in my food."

"She needs a ribbon." Briefly Alec allowed his gaze to rest on Kimberly. His smile said, *I'll bring you one.* At noon, he did just that.

Kimberly drew back her long hair and tied it with the narrow satin strip, saying nothing. She could not endure another meal fraught with unsaid things and unstated messages. She left Alec to her aunt and fled downtown. She had manufactured an errand for herself.

Away from the house she felt somewhat calmer. Good heaven, the man filled her with so many emotions it made her dizzy. With a sinking sensation, she wondered if she were falling in love with him. What a joke that would be, she thought grimly. It would prove she'd been a perfect fool about Roger, who now seemed as dim and inconsequential as a childhood dream.

And if this was love, she thought, why did it have to feel so frightening? The sensation was so strong it was terrifying. She imagined it was like walking on a high wire, knowing there was no net beneath. For while Alec's eyes and Alec's smiles had told her all sorts of wonderful things this morning, all he had ever actually said was that he wanted her. Not cared for her in the least.

She also tried not to think of a darker side she sensed in Alec. He'd locked his room again this morning. One of the few things he had actually said to her was an express order not to go inside.

"I don't want you and your aunt going to so much trouble." He had smiled. But behind the smile had been that same hard-faced and brooding expression she'd seen on his face in the garden that morning.

Although the sun spilled down friendly light on the winding brick streets, and the familiar eccentric buildings basked in the warmth, Kimberly felt uneasy, as if she were walking through a new and dangerous territory. She didn't have a map of it, and she didn't know its rules.

THAT EVENING, her uneasiness took even stronger hold. It was one of the long, bright blue twilights of the mountains, almost luminous in its beauty. They all sat on the front porch once again, sipping sherry, watching the hummingbirds hover dreamlike around the flowering quince.

Calvin had dropped by and sat on the stairs, softly strumming his mandolin. He played no particular tune and could not be induced to sing. The sunset, he claimed, was upstaging him. He was oddly quiet, almost shy, once he arrived.

Conversation was quiet. Lazily Alec asked questions about the old times and Dodo answered in her breathy voice. But in spite of the peaceful atmosphere, Kimberly sensed all sorts of strange tensions and expectations in the hazy air.

Lela Munroe, in tight white shorts and high-heeled sandals, sat in one of the cobra-back wicker chairs. She wore a white shirt with a plunging neckline and the tails tied around her bare waist. She, too, asked questions of Dodo, but impatiently, as if she wished Alec would lose interest in the past and pay attention to her. Lela watched him hungrily, like a cat secretly determined to satisfy its appetite.

"Well, how exactly did this rajah finally die?" Lela demanded, sounding bored. It was a rude question, for Dodo had delicately avoided the details of the long-ago crime.

"Oh," Dodo said uncomfortably. She clasped her fingers together in her lap. "It happened in his gem room. A blow to the head. Struck in anger, no doubt," she said sadly.

Alec stretched his long legs. He wore jeans and a blue chambray shirt with the sleeves rolled up to reveal his forearms. Once again he wore tall boots, and they gleamed in the fading light. He sat casually beside Kimberly on the swing, but she could feel his presence as powerfully as if he were a man made out of electricity.

He stretched his arm nonchalantly, draping it over the back of the swing so that his fingers almost touched her bare shoulder. She wore a blue sundress this evening. His fingers, so near her skin, radiated a warmth that made her feel chill everywhere else.

"Gem room?" he asked lackadaisically. But he gave Kimberly a brief, sidewise glance that crackled with suppressed intensity. The excitement he stirred in her made her look away.

"The rajah had a special room for his gems," Dodo explained dutifully. "No servant was allowed inside. The only other person with a key was my father. He was the only one the rajah trusted." There was pride in her voice.

Calvin strummed lyrical chords and stole a long glance at Dodo sitting in the twilight.

"So the old British advisor just sneaked in and bashed him on the head and killed him, hmm?" Lela asked, clearly anxious to get the story done with. "I hear there's a dance band at one of the hotels tonight," she said brightly, smiling at Alec. "Anybody interested?"

He smiled politely but said nothing. His hand moved a fraction of an inch closer to Kimberly's shoulder.

Dodo was obviously disturbed by Lela's crude summation. "Oh, it wasn't like *that*," she said, eyes wide. "The advisor was staying in the palace—it was festival time. He asked for a private audience about the copper mines. They met in the gem room. They must have quarreled—for Sir Cyril was seen storming out of the gem room. And the door was left unlocked. My father came in to find the rajah— gone from us."

"And the great topaz stolen?" Alec questioned. "The Heart of the Sun gone?"

Dodo nodded unhappily and stared into her lap.

Calvin looked up from his mandolin, studying her carefully. He fingered his handlebar mustache thoughtfully. "Maybe you shouldn't talk about it if it upsets you, Miss Dodo."

Dodo clasped her hands more tightly together. "Oh," she sighed, "it was such a long time ago. I can talk about it—now."

Although on the surface Alec seemed relaxed, Kimberly sensed tension in his lean body. "And who, precisely, saw Sir Cyril leave the gem room?" he asked. He offered the question casually, but there was something in his voice.

Dodo had taken out her lacy handkerchief and was twisting it. "Why, the servants," she said. "Three of them. And," she added softly, "me." Her voice dropped until the last word was almost inaudible.

"You?" Alec asked. "You actually saw him leaving?"

"This may have happened long ago," Calvin observed grimly, "but it obviously isn't pleasant for Miss Dodo to talk about—"

"I *don't* mind, really," Dodo protested, but her voice was strained. "After all, I testified at the trial. Yes, I saw him. I saw his back. I recognized his uniform. A blue frock coat trimmed with gold, a white helmet with a golden spike, and a long sword that curved... I saw it all quite clearly. I—I didn't want to testify. But my father said it was my duty. So I did."

"And why," Alec persisted, "did you happen to be near the gem room?"

Dodo twisted her handkerchief unhappily. "To meet my father—I thought. He was to take me for an elephant ride. But I was a flibbertigibbet even then. I had the time wrong.

So instead I saw—what I saw. And for more than forty years I've wished I hadn't.''

"But you did, and that's that," Lela Munroe said, trying to put an end to reminiscences. "No need to dwell on it. My, the stars are coming out. They seem so bright here—not like in the city. Are the stars bright in Australia, Alec?''

"Very bright indeed," Alec said noncommittally. His tone became somewhat gentler. "I'm sorry if my questions upset you, Miss Simpson. I was curious, that's all. It's a flaw of mine."

"Oh, it's no fault, Mr. Shaughnessy," Dodo insisted, but the quaver remained in her voice. "It would be a far greater flaw to have no curiosity at all."

"I'm curious about Australia," Lela Munroe said sweetly. "Won't you tell us about it, Alec? What's it like?''

"I fear my poor words wouldn't do it justice," Alec said. Darkness had thickened now, and he let his fingertips just touch Kimberly's shoulder. She sat as still as stone, but the contact made unbidden feelings rush through her.

"Australia's full of unusual things," Calvin said, taking charge of the conversation. He cast a worried look at Dodo, who still seemed sad, lost deep in the past. "Wallabies. Kangaroos. And Qantas bears.''

"Koala bears," Alec corrected, his forefinger discreetly touching a loose tendril of Kimberly's hair.

"Koala bears," amended Calvin. He plucked out the opening strains of a melody on his mandolin, then sang a rollicking song about a man and a bear having a drinking contest. By its end Dodo was laughing again, pressing her lacy handkerchief against her mouth as if she were a child who wasn't supposed to laugh at such naughtiness.

"I know another one," Calvin said, smiling up at her. "It's about a 'possum and a preacher and a sweet potato pie." He sang again and seemed to glow when Dodo smiled.

How odd everything is, thought Kimberly, her heart beating so hard it hurt. She had realized only tonight that Calvin adored Dodo; had, perhaps, for years. And Dodo, of course, was both too innocent and too modest to have any inkling.

Lela Munroe tapped her high-heeled slipper to Calvin's song, but out of the corner of her eye, she still watched Alec. Dodo did not see that, either, and Calvin was probably too caught up with Dodo to notice. And none of the others knew that, under the cover of the darkness, Alec's fingertips secretly toyed with the blue ribbon in Kimberly's hair. The golden light from the street lamp fell in such a way as to keep his hand in shadow, but Kimberly could feel his secret touch, feel it all through her body.

They all sat quietly, almost languidly on the darkening porch. But beneath the placid surface of appearances, all sorts of hidden forces surged. Unseen emotions circled around them more thickly than the pale moths that winged about the street lamp.

Calvin finished his tune, and Lela Munroe applauded brightly. "Bravo," she cried. "If music be the food of love, play on." Calvin simply looked embarrassed.

Alec stretched, then drawled, "Think I'll take a walk. Perhaps to the park. Would you care to join me, Kimberly?"

Her emotions fluttered in happy excitement. It was the first time he had ever used her given name in front of the others. And she knew he wanted to be alone with her, to talk to her in private. Her apparent calm amazed her. "Yes. Thank you."

He gave her blue ribbon one last, slightly irreverent secret tug and smiled at her through the darkness.

Then Lela Munroe said, "I think I'll come, too, if you don't mind. I could stretch my legs."

"I'll come, too," Calvin said uncomfortably. He set his hat on his bald head, adjusting it just so. He was self-conscious about being left alone with Dodo, Kimberly decided.

"Then I'll just tidy up," Dodo said, oblivious to the dramas playing around her. "Thanks for the serenade, Mr. Calvin."

Calvin rose, joining the others, and tipped his hat to her. The four of them strolled down the maple-lined street.

"We look like a bloody parade," Alec managed to whisper in Kimberly's ear. He did not so much as take her hand in front of Calvin and Lela.

Yet Kimberly felt as if they were somehow touching. Even when they returned to the house, and Lela Munroe stayed determinedly at Alec's side, Kimberly had the odd conviction that she and Alec reached out to each other, communicating without words.

It was obvious that Lela Munroe was not going to leave the two of them alone. Alec walked Kimberly inside the house. At the foot of the stairs he gave her an ironic, private smile. He excused himself and went up to bed. Lela gave Kimberly a brisk and unfriendly "good-night" and immediately followed him.

Kimberly stood at the foot of the stairs, her hand on the newel post. She and Alec had been alone only once today, early this morning. That seemed centuries ago. There had been so little time to say anything.

"Are you happy?" he had asked her in the bright new light of day.

And she had said, "Yes."

She put her hand to the blue ribbon he'd brought her. It was the simplest of ribbons, but it seemed suddenly more precious to her than any treasure her grandfather had ever had from the rajah.

What she had told Alec was the truth. For the first time in her life she was deeply and completely happy. She did not even understand why. She only knew that she was so happy that it ought to last forever.

At last she, too, went to bed. The house was silent, but she had trouble falling asleep. She lay alone in the darkness, staring out the window at the stars.

Down the hall, lying fully clothed on his bed, Alec Shaughnessy, too, was far from asleep. He frowned at the ceiling and ran his hand restlessly over his upper lip.

Damn, he thought. A little more time in the attic, and he hoped to have the answer to part of the puzzle. And the women, both the aunt and Kimberly, were in his power now.

The aunt had told him almost freely about the rajah's death and what she'd witnessed. How odd. For years he had heard the story, only not quite the way she had told it. And how differently he'd always imagined Dodo—he'd always fancied her as sharp-eyed, conniving, self-satisfied. She was none of those. She was actually most likable. He hadn't counted on that.

He hadn't counted on Kimberly, either. She had caught him off guard and badly. It was maddening. Everyone, including himself, was caught up in the old stories of the past. Of all concerned, she alone seemed a creature of the present, a disturbing creature.

The way she could look at him, at once so eager and so hesitant, so wary yet so brave, made something go slightly insane in his blood. He stirred restlessly and swore under his breath.

If she came to his door, to his bed now, he would throw away all caution for the future. But she wouldn't. She was too proud for that—and too new to the ancient and complicated game of desire. Her innocence, he thought, her be-wildering innocence. It would be either his salvation or his undoing.

CHAPTER FIVE

THE NEXT DAY was one of those days so seemingly cursed that nothing went right. Rain didn't simply fall, it coursed down in unceasing streams.

Lela Munroe could not go shopping nor could she lie in the backyard and work on her tan. She brooded around the house like an evil presence. Nothing could amuse or satisfy her.

Alec had left early, braving the driving rain for some appointment. Two more guests arrived, a pair of middle-aged sisters who immediately began to complain that the weather was ruining their vacation. Dodo had just mollified everyone and got them to sit down to watch television while she baked cookies, when lightning struck a power line. Both the television and the oven went out.

The wind blew so hard that two large limbs blew off the catalpa tree and a loose window screen crashed from the second story and lay twisted in the rose bed. Water backed up in the basement drain, gurgling sinisterly. Water dripped from the ceiling of the upstairs hall, and Kimberly feared that shingles had blown off. She put down a bucket to catch the drips and tried to call a repair man. The phone was out of order.

Dodo was almost beside herself.

"We should have gone to Florida," said Miss Freda Fremont, one of the sisters.

"We should have stayed in Iowa," said Miss Mona Fremont, the other sister, the one with the glasses. "We certainly should have never come *here*."

"I should have stayed at a hotel," complained Lela Munroe. "I think we should get a discount on our rate. We don't even have electricity here."

"Would anyone like to play bridge?" Dodo asked with desperate enthusiasm.

"I despise bridge," sniffed Miss Freda Fremont.

"*I* consider cards a waste of time," Miss Mona Fremont said with great superiority.

"I'm an expert bridge player," put in Lela Munroe. "I do not play at *amateur* bridge."

It was at this moment that lightning struck the outside spigot, the one used to water the back garden. Thunder deafened everyone and the whole house shook, smelling slightly of brimstone.

"Eek!" screamed both Fremont sisters.

"What now?" demanded Lela. "Is nature going to strike us all dead, or what? Should I just go out and lie in the yard so the lightning has a better shot at me?"

"Nothing like this has ever happened before," Dodo stated, sounding badly rattled. "I swear."

Kimberly ran into the backyard to examine the damage. At first it seemed minimal. Then she realized that somehow the force of the lightning bolt had turned the spigot so the water was on and could not be shut off. The faucet seemed welded permanently into the "on" position.

The water gushed out energetically, flowed down the slope a bit and then directly into the cracked basement window. Kimberly had visions of the house being borne off in a flood of its own making, an ark without a captain.

She ran inside and down into the basement. She stared in dismay at the water coming in, now, through both the bad drain and the window.

Dashing back upstairs, she snatched her raincoat out of the hall closet.

"Kimberly!" Dodo cried, "you're drenched! You can't go out in this—what do you think you're doing?"

"I'm going to find a plumber," Kimberly asserted. She pushed her wet hair back out of her eyes. "And I'll do the shopping for lunch. You stay here and hold the fort."

"But—" protested Dodo.

"Dodo," Kimberly said, her eyes flushing, "I have the easy job—you have to stay here with the three demons of the storm. I'm not brave enough." She nodded significantly toward the dining room, where Lela Munroe was grumbling and the Fremont sisters were alternately moaning and complaining.

"Oh, *dear!*" said Dodo. "It's a good thing the colonel can't see this."

He'd kick all three of them down the stairs and out into the rain, Kimberly thought with grim satisfaction as she dashed out the door and toward her blue Ford compact. Hell, she was certain, was a large and disorderly inn that the benighted had to maintain.

Every plumber in town seemed to be out of his shop, but Kimberly was told that one was at a downtown hotel. She could catch him if she was lucky.

She entered the lobby of the little Half Moon Hotel, but the only people she saw were the bored desk clerk and Calvin, who sat in an old armchair doing a crossword puzzle and looking discontented. His face lit up when he saw her.

"Kimberly!" he grinned. "Out for a swim? Come have a cup of coffee with me. This weather has ruined the minstrel business."

She tried to shake the rain from her hair but knew she was thoroughly sodden. "I can't, Calvin, I have to find Fred Merkle. We need a plumber—badly."

"You missed him," Calvin stated. "Don't know where he went."

"Oh, no," Kimberly wailed.

"What do you need him for? Maybe I can help. I can do a little plumbing."

"Oh, Calvin, do you think you could?" Kimberly explained the problem as best she could.

"Sure," Calvin shrugged modestly. "I'll just shut down the pipe. I'll get my tools. But first," he said firmly, "we have coffee. Every man has his price, and that's mine. Coffee with a fresh young face on a stormy old day."

"Calvin," Kimberly said with gratitude. "You're wonderful." She had almost forgotten that Calvin earned his room in the hotel by keeping up small repairs. In winter he served as the unofficial assistant caretaker.

He ushered her into the small coffee shop, hung up her raincoat for her and made her sit down.

"You're going to look like a delivering angel to Dodo," she said.

He gave her a wry look. "It'd take more than a stuck faucet repair to make me look like an angel." He patted his bald head, then twirled his big mustache. "I'm just an old ne'er-do-well. But at least I'm handy."

When the steaming coffee came, it seemed like ambrosia to Kimberly. Calvin looked at her thoughtfully.

"Sweet Kim," he began. "You are my favorite cupcake, you know..."

"Uh-oh," Kimberly smiled. "Flattery. That must mean you're up to something."

"Nope." He stuck his thumbs under his suspenders and leaned back in his chair. "It means I wonder if you're falling for that Aussie."

Kimberly blinked hard. Her coffee cup, halfway to her lips, halted in midair. "What?" she asked, so startled she felt nearly numb.

"You heard me," he said, scrutinizing her with fatherly interest.

Oh, good heaven, Kimberly thought, managing to get her cup to her mouth and take a warming sip. Did it show? She thought she had acted with such perfect normalcy in Alec's presence. Had she instead been so obvious?

"I'm not falling for anyone," she muttered. *Liar,* said her conscience.

"Good," returned Calvin. "I'm not sure I trust him. I don't like the way he kept after Dodo about that old story. He upset her."

"Oh," she said with false lightness, "I see. It's Dodo you're worried about. Is that why you came around last night—to check on her?"

"Maybe partly," he replied evasively. "But Shaughnessy was in here this morning, know that? Using the pay phone at 8:00 a.m. Saw him in the booth. He took a long time, and he didn't look happy. Looked even unhappier when he saw me. Why didn't he use the phone at your place?"

Kimberly shrugged and tried not to wonder. Alec had a right to privacy, she told herself righteously, the same as anyone else.

"At any rate," Calvin continued shyly, "I thought you were supposed to be broken-hearted over some fool in Kansas City. You don't have to fall in love every week. Even if you are young enough to do it."

Rebuked, she fought back a blush. Calvin was saying what everyone would think if they knew the truth. "You're a great one to talk," she countered. "I never knew until last night that you had a great big crush on my aunt."

"Right," he answered, not daunted in the least. "And the reason you never knew is because I'm old enough not to wear my heart on my sleeve. I'm also old enough to know my own mind and to be a pretty good judge of character."

"And I'm not?" she challenged.

"No, sweet stuff," he said with total conviction. "You're not."

"And just what deep dark dismal character flaw do you think Alec Shaughnessy is hiding?" she asked, trying to conceal her hurt.

"I don't know. Maybe it's not even exactly a flaw. It's just a feeling I've got. So be careful, all right?"

"Oh, good grief," she said irritably. But she couldn't make herself meet Calvin's pale eyes and so instead stared into her empty coffee cup. "What makes you think I'm not careful?"

"The fact that you're you," he replied. "You feel too much, and you feel it too hard. You have since you were knee-high to a grasshopper. Your grandfather couldn't scare it out of you, and Dodo couldn't train it out of you. I don't want to see life crush it out of you. I got an interest in you, kiddo."

She looked up at him. He was perfectly serious for once. He sat with his big arms crossed, regarding her gravely. She swallowed hard, feeling suddenly young, inexperienced and overwhelmed by complexities. "You really care about her a lot, don't you?" she asked softly. "About Dodo. Don't you?"

"In my way, kid. In my way. Now let's get rolling. I got pipes to fix and you got groceries to buy."

KIMBERLY RETURNED to the house shortly after eleven in the morning. She made her way from the car through the downpour, clutching bags of groceries.

Dodo greeted her at the door, fussing mightily. "How did you ever come up with the idea of Calvin?" Dodo asked, brushing Kimberly's wet hair back from her cheek. "You've always been so resourceful, Kimberly, I just marvel at you. And at him. He seems to be able to do anything. He shut off the pipe and he fixed the drain, and he insists, as soon as the rain stops, that he'll fix the shingles and the window screen. Right now he's repairing that loose basement step."

Kimberly could hear the sound of a hammer banging away. Ah, Dodo, she thought, you've got a devoted cavalier and don't even suspect it.

"The electricity's back on, thank heaven," Dodo said, rolling her eyes in gratitude. "I've got a fresh bunch of clean sheets out of the dryer. Can you do the beds while I make lunch? But first, get out of those wet clothes, dear girl."

Carefully Kimberly carried the sheets upstairs and set them on the hall table, trying to keep the rain in her hair from falling on them.

She stared at Alec's closed door. He had locked it again this morning, saying he would remake his own bed. But, she wondered, shouldn't she check inside, just in case? What if the ceiling in his room were leaking, too? Surely it wouldn't be wrong to open the door just to see.

She stood before the door, doubts assailing her. Once again she thought of the legend of Bluebeard and the locked, forbidden room. She remembered Calvin's warning, that he didn't trust Alec Shaughnessy and that she should be careful. What, she thought, did she actually know about this handsome stranger who had set her world topsy-turvy? Nothing. She thought, too, of the mysterious Indian box in his drawer with Ganesha on its lid. It, too, was locked.

But, she told herself gamely, all she was really wondering was if the rain were leaking inside the room. Didn't she have the right, even the duty to look?

Softly she ran back downstairs and got the spare key. Moments later she stood before Alec's door once more, her heart beating hard. She inserted the key in the lock. She turned it quietly.

She paused a moment. From downstairs she could hear the blare of the television and the banging of Calvin's hammer. The wind still wailed about the house, crying like a banshee. She put her hand on the knob and turned it.

"Hullo, what's this?" said a voice near her ear. She jumped slightly, just as a cool hand closed over her wrist. "Didn't I tell you not to go in?"

Kimberly wheeled. She stared up into the sapphire eyes of Alec Shaughnessy. His hair was dark with the rain, and drops glittered on the shoulders of his raincoat. He kept his hand firmly encircling her wrist.

"The rain," she almost gasped. "The house is leaking— I wanted to check—" She nodded toward the bucket standing in the hallway. He looked at the water descending from the ceiling in steady drops.

He turned his attention back to her, smiling down, his smile slightly askew. "A leak? Well, let's check." He opened the door and ushered her into the room before him. He closed the door. They both stared wordlessly at the ceiling for a moment.

"Well," Kimberly said at last, clearing her throat. "Everything seems in order. You should be as nice and dry as toast in here."

She turned to go, but looked up into his eyes and did not move away.

"You've the rain in your hair again," he breathed.

She nodded. "You, too," she replied softly. She wanted to reach out and touch his cheekbones, which still shone with moisture. She didn't resist when he moved toward her and put his hands lightly on her arms. Although her flesh was warmed now, his was still icy cold from the rain. She shivered pleasurably.

"For the rest of my life," he said, drawing her nearer, "will the perfume of the rain make me think of you? And will you come haunting me forever, a beautiful little ghost with dark eyes and mermaid hair?"

He expected no answer and waited for none. Instead his lips descended slowly to her waiting ones. He folded her more tightly into his arms. His mouth was at first cool, then warm upon her own. The rain on his mustache moistened her upper lip, and his tongue took the errant drop away, then moved against hers, tasting as intimately as he could.

His hands were tangled in her long hair now. Her arms were around his neck.

She could feel the wet roughness of his raincoat, and his chest pressed hard against her breasts. His hands moved to her face, tilting it further up and holding it so he could kiss her again and yet again.

With a gruff sigh, he opened his raincoat, and unbuttoned first his shirt, then her blouse, without taking his lips from hers. Then his arms wrapped her around again, and their rain-damp bodies strained to touch more completely.

His hands moved to explore the smooth satin planes of her back, and his mouth pressed against her throat.

"Kimberly," he said harshly. He drew back, staring down at her, his gaze so heated he almost frightened her. She stood, her blouse unbuttoned and parted, her long hair falling over the delicate pink silk that covered her breasts.

"Look at you," he whispered, eyes taking in her half nakedness. "A body more beautiful than any jewel. I should take you to some island where you should never have to wear clothes at all, but go about dressed only in the veils of your hair."

Suddenly shy with him she looked away, shaking her head so that her hair swept to hide her scantily clad breasts more completely. Then she raised her eyes to his again. He smiled at her and taking the sheltering tresses in his hands, he moved them so that they spilled down her back instead.

"Alec," she murmured desperately. "We can't do this. There's a houseful of people downstairs. It's the middle of the day—"

"I know, love. I know too well."

His hands ran lightly down her arms, settled beneath her blouse on her bare waist. "But I need to touch you. Hold you. For just a moment."

Almost trembling, she put her slender hands against the musculature of his chest where his shirt parted.

"And let me look at you," he said, staring down intently at her. "A moment longer. That's all. For I swear, I'd rather hold you, like this, than have all the opals of Australia running through my hands."

He bent and kissed the swell of each breast, at the velvety line where her tan ended. Then he straightened and, gazing into her wide dark eyes, draped her hair so that it hid her partial nakedness once more.

Then he paused and kissed her lingeringly behind the ear. His hands gripped her shoulders. "You," he breathed in her ear, "You…" His hands moved to her arms, and he turned her to face him again. His face was almost somber as he slowly buttoned her blouse up.

He kissed her on the lips again. "Go to your room, love," he said. "And put yourself in order. You're rosy, and I've taken all your lipstick away. You look all too clearly like a woman who's been kissed."

He watched as she lifted her hand and buttoned the buttons of his shirt back up. He took her hand and kissed the palm. His mustache grazed the base of her fingers, making them tremble.

"You," he said again and let her go.

Quickly she moved to the door and let herself out. She fled down the hall to her own room. Had it only been an hour ago, she wondered, that Calvin warned her against the danger of her own too-powerful emotions and of trusting Alec Shaughnessy?

She looked into her mirror. Her guilt showed this time. With her clinging blouse, long tousled hair and tenderly swollen lips, she did indeed look like a woman who had been kissed. And wished to be kissed again.

When she went downstairs at last, she found that Calvin had been invited to stay for lunch. Kimberly sat down at the table across from Alec, trying to act casually, as if nothing had happened. Alec gave her the slightest of smiles. She barely acknowledged it.

But Calvin, she knew, saw. He looked at Kimberly, then Alec, then Kimberly again. He shook his head in grief or disgust or both.

To Dodo's consternation, Alec spent the rest of the afternoon fixing the damage in the attic. Calvin offered to help, but Alec turned him down. "Can't let you do all the good deeds, mate," he said. "Besides, I started it. May as well finish it." Calvin gathered his tools and went back to the hotel. The rain had almost stopped.

"You and your aunt certainly get the men to do your bidding," Lela Munroe said unpleasantly. She sat at the dining room table playing solitaire and watching Kimberly polish the silverware. "I'm surprised you do any of your own work. It must be that helpless act your aunt puts on."

"My aunt," retorted Kimberly, "has never put on an act in her life. And she's far from helpless. She raised me single-handed, and she cared for my grandfather until the end, and she started this business all by herself."

"Well," replied Lela airily, "you needn't get touchy. She has her methods, and I see that you have yours. But yours are very different."

"Different?" Kimberly asked, burnishing a spoon and closing one eye to inspect its shine.

"Yes," Lela returned, slapping a red queen on a black king. "Acting so uppity with Alec Shaughnessy, trying to get him interested. You'll do yourself more harm than good, you know."

Kimberly set down the spoon and turned her scrutiny to Lela Munroe. The woman's flyaway blond hair made an untidy frame for her smug face. "I beg your pardon," she said crisply.

"A man like him," Lela said with a skewering smile, "would only want a little slip of a thing like you for one reason."

"Meaning?" Kimberly demanded.

"Meaning," Lela answered, gathering up her cards and stacking them neatly, "if he does pay you any notice, it certainly won't be your mind that he's interested in. Or your personality. Such as it is."

She set the cards down neatly on the edge of the table, then deliberately knocked them off. They showered to the floor.

"Oops," said Lela, giving Kimberly the same little puckered smile. "That should keep you out of trouble. For a little while."

She stood and drifted into the living room where the Fremont sisters were sulkily watching an old Cary Grant movie.

Dodo came into the dining room, adjusting her lavender apron. "Why, Kimberly," she said, her eyes widening. "Whatever's the matter? Your cheeks are so pink you look feverish. And how did these cards get all over the floor?"

"Nothing's wrong," Kimberly said sharply. "And don't touch those cards. I'll pick them up." She rose and went to the scattered deck, kneeling down to gather them so that Dodo wouldn't have to.

Good grief, Kimberly thought darkly. First Calvin warned her, then Lela Munroe, of all people. Perhaps everyone in the world would line up outside the door when the rain was over and they could all warn her about Alec Shaughnessy, each and every one of them. But Lela was a woman of the world. Was she right? Did Alec only want one thing from her?

She picked up the last card, the ace of spades, and put it face up on top of the deck. Her cheeks, she hoped, had returned to normal color again, her angry heart slowed to a more rational beat.

"Oh," said Dodo with a genteel shudder. "The ace of spades. The bad luck card. Don't put that one on top, dear. Hide it away from the light of day—somewhere in the middle."

"It's only superstition," Kimberly countered. But it occurred to her that superstition, fortune both good and bad, was the very stuff of Alec's occupation.

She picked up the deck, the black ace still on top. She walked absently into the kitchen and looked out the window. The rain had stopped at last. The sun was showing in the west, trying to break through the clouds over the mountains. Cheerily and with almost unnatural beauty, a rainbow arched on the horizon.

A rainbow meant good luck, didn't it? she thought. She stood, with a symbol of ill fortune in one hand, staring out at a symbol of good fortune. She wondered, fearfully, which forecast the shape of her future.

UPSTAIRS, in the dim and dusty stuffiness of the attic, Alec sat, his elbow on his knee, staring down at the last of the papers he had unearthed. His face was grave, and the disturbance in his blue eyes was great. He shook his head hopelessly, rubbing a meditative hand across his chin.

He could not take his gaze away from the colonel's records, the yellowing paper with its crabbed handwriting, the old reports. Damn him, Alec thought bitterly, damn the old fox to hell. He thought of Kimberly and shook his head again. Things were worse than he thought. Far worse.

He would have to resort to desperate actions. He had no choice. God help us all, he thought.

CHAPTER SIX

THAT EVENING Alec went out, not saying where. Lela Munroe set off for where the nightlife was liveliest. The Fremont sisters departed for the music theater, complaining of dampness in the air. Dodo, exhausted by the rigors of the day, went to bed early.

Kimberly sat moodily on the love seat in the living room, sketching. The lamplight fell in a golden circle about her and glittered on the rough crystals of the fireplace. Her pencil seemed to have a will of its own and wanted only to draw Alec's face.

Unhappily she scribbled a line that obscured the portrait. She turned to a fresh page and began to try once more to sketch a white squirrel. But her thoughts dwelt on Alec.

When he'd descended from the attic that afternoon, he had seemed thoughtful, serious, even distant, as if something weighed heavily on his mind. Absently, he'd assured Dodo that everything was in order now, and once the shingles were repaired there would be no more invasions by rambunctious squirrels.

He had cast Kimberly a look that haunted her still. His face had been hard, almost cold, but he'd smiled at her. There'd been something so mocking in the smile that it jolted her even now. It was almost as if he'd been telling her goodbye without words. Not good-night, but goodbye. Then he'd left.

Now he was gone, why or where, she didn't know. She did not want to recall the incident in his room. It filled her with conflicts, sharp yearning mingled with shame. It seemed that every time the two of them were alone, it was impossible that he not take her in his arms. It was just as impossible for her to resist. It was, she thought bitterly, like being under a curse.

Calvin was right—her emotions were too headlong. She had thought she felt strongly about Roger, but in a short time, Alec had made those feelings seem as insubstantial as shadows. He had taken her across new borders of both pleasure and fear. He had introduced her to an unknown country of emotion, vast and treacherous.

She could have sworn he was avoiding her tonight. She was half-wounded, half-grateful. If he wasn't here, he couldn't put her under the spell of his strange magic. Perhaps Lela Munroe, too, was right. A man like Alec could have no permanent interest in someone like Kimberly.

The front door opened, and she stiffened, wondering if it were Alec. It was, instead, the Fremont sisters, returning from the theater. They seemed in slightly better moods.

"Good evening," said Freda Fremont, fluffing her reddish curls. "We had a splendid time. It almost redeemed this wretched day."

"It's about time something went right," observed Mona Fremont. Like her sister, she had gingery hair, freckles, and a sharp, birdlike nose. She wore green-rimmed glasses with rhinestones glittering on the corners. "This is an interesting house," Mona continued, her eyes darting around the room. "But I was certain it was going to fall in on us during that storm."

"I don't think so," Kimberly assured her, adding a stroke to her sketch. "My grandfather built this place to last."

"Yes," answered Mona, still peering over her rhinestones to appraise the room. "But he must have been an odd
duck." She adjusted her glasses and stared at some of the
knickknacks Dodo had set on pieces of quartz that jutted
out like natural shelves.

"You have a great many pieces from Thailand or someplace," she said, examining an etched brass bell. She picked
it up and jingled it.

"India," Kimberly corrected. "My grandfather spent
time in India."

"Wherever," Mona shrugged. She replaced the bell then
put her hands on either side of the black enameled vase with
its brass lid. "Now this is rather nice," she said conde-
scendingly. "What's this?"

Kimberly looked at the two of them, poking and finger-
ing all of Dodo's objects. Freda was critically regarding the
brass bell now, and Mona was turning the vase to see the rest
of its gold design. "That," Kimberly said with wicked satisfaction, "is Grandfather."

"What?" Mona Fremont's hands went still on the vase,
and her voice had turned icy.

"That," Kimberly repeated calmly, "is Grandfather. His
ashes. He saved that vase for years. He used to say, 'I don't
intend to die. I'll just change forms, like a genie, and go into
this jar.' And there he is."

Mona Fremont made a horrid gurgling sound in her
throat. Her hands flew away from the vase and she began
wiping them madly on the ample bosom of her dotted dress.
"You have a dead person on your fireplace!" she accused,
glaring through her rhinestone-encrusted glasses at Kimberly.

"Lots of people keep the ashes of their loved ones,"
Kimberly answered coolly. "You get used to the idea."

"*I* wouldn't," Mona insisted, still wiping her hands.

"I, for one, will try to forget I ever heard such a ghastly fact," Freda stated, her sharp little nose in the air. "Really, this place is too eccentric."

"Come, Freda," Mona said, shaking her head. "Let's go to bed. We need rest. We've had a trying day."

"We certainly have, Mona," Freda answered. "Good night, Kimmery."

"Kimberly," Kimberly corrected sweetly. "Good night, ladies. Sleep well."

They plodded upstairs, and the house lapsed into silence again. Once more Kimberly felt Alec's absence, and it left her empty and panged. She finished her sketch, then went up to bed herself, but had trouble sleeping. She heard Lela Munroe come in, and from the stumbling, bumping and fumbling noises at her door, she decided the woman sounded tipsy.

It was after three in the morning when Kimberly finally heard Alec return. Where could he have been, she wondered wearily. Almost every place had been closed for hours. She heard him pause outside her door. She held her breath. If he came in, if he reached to her through the darkness, what would she do?

But after a long moment, she heard his footsteps moving on, his own door opening, then closing.

THE SUNSHINE seemed especially brilliant the next morning, as if it were trying to make up for the dreariness of the day before. There were bluebirds in the garden this year, and they sang in celebration. The rain had shattered most of the open roses, but new ones were unfolding to the sun.

Kimberly stood by the kitchen window, washing a few dishes. Alec had risen late, and Dodo had made him a special breakfast. Now she was upstairs, stripping the beds. The other guests had gone out for the day. Alec had said nothing more than "Good morning" to Kimberly when Dodo had been there.

Now she sensed his presence behind her. He put his arms around her waist, nuzzled her hair away from her throat and kissed her just below the ear. His touch made her go alarmingly cold all over and she shivered slightly. She did not respond to him because she was afraid to.

"You ought to be outlawed," he growled, his voice strained. "I can't see you without wanting you in my arms. What's a man to do? The sunshine makes amber jewels shine in your hair, did you know?"

"No," she answered, feeling a shudder of desire as he kissed the back of her neck. She forced herself to hold very still. "Don't do that," she said as his lips moved back to her ear.

"I told you. I have to. You've bewitched me. The fault is yours."

Kimberly's patience broke. She thrust his hands away from her waist. Freeing herself from his embrace, she turned, staring up at him. "The fault *is* mine," she said curtly. "For letting you. I want this stopped. I—I'm tired of it. It's like you're the king of the castle and I'm the serving maid. You think you can just—grab me, any time."

For a moment there had been a trace of laughter in his eyes. It died. His mouth quirked bitterly beneath his mustache. "Is that how you see it?"

"Exactly," she replied, although she was no longer sure how she saw anything. Still, she thought, there was justice in her charge. Alec was cold one moment, seductive the next. He came and went as he pleased, and had never done more than ask her for a walk. Roger, at least, had the decency to take her out before he tried to get her into his bed. "And I want you to stop," she asserted. She raised her chin in defiance, but in truth it was her own weakness she was defying.

"Do you?" His voice was sarcastic. He folded his arms across his chest, and the look on his face was far from kind.

"Yes. I do." But her voice quavered slightly.

He took a step toward her. He put his hand out, gathering her hair at the back of her neck. The movement forced her face to tilt up toward his. The curve of his mouth grew more cynical. "Liar," he whispered.

He bent and kissed her, briefly but very hard. He drew back when he heard Dodo's footsteps on the stairs. He kept her hair imprisoned, her face turned up to his. "Liar," he whispered again harshly. He smiled a one-cornered smile, then released her, turning on his heel and leaving the kitchen.

She stared after him in confused alarm. Dodo entered, carrying the laundry basket. "Goodness, Kimberly," she said, setting down the basket and patting her niece's face affectionately. "Your cheeks are pink as roses again. Are you sure you're all right?"

"I'm fine," Kimberly lied.

KIMBERLY WAS GLAD that Lela Munroe had gone out that morning. She would have viewed events with too much gleeful malice. First, Calvin showed up, resplendent in clean jeans and red suspenders, carrying his tool kit. He claimed he had a sore throat, so singing was impossible for the next day or so. If Dodo would give him a few more meals like the one yesterday, he would use his time to make repairs on the house.

Dodo blushed and fluttered and protested but finally gave in. Then Alec confounded both Dodo and Kimberly by saying he'd stay around and help Calvin. He'd taken in so much information, he claimed, so many notes, he needed time to mull it over. He'd like to work with his hands to help clear his mind, he said.

"I couldn't!" Dodo almost wailed. "I couldn't allow it!"

He smiled down at her. "You must allow it. It's my special request, and you can't be unkind enough to deny it."

"Everyone is so good," Dodo said emotionally. Tears filled her eyes. "My father always claimed that everyone in the world was out for something, but it's not true. You two are so exceptionally good to us."

Calvin looked slightly guilty.

As for Alec Shaughnessy, he showed no glimmer of emotion. "It's my pleasure" was all he said.

Later Dodo made Kimberly take a glass of lemonade to Alec, who was working in the basement. Dodo herself bore one to Calvin, who was outside, rehanging a screen window.

Kimberly went down the steep steps with trepidation. She wanted no more confrontations with Alec. She wished he'd gone off, doing whatever it was he usually did.

"I don't know what you're up to," she said, handing him the glass and backing away slightly.

Dust smudged his forehead, and he wiped it away with the back of his hand. His hair fell into his eyes, and his work shirt and jeans were covered with cobwebs. "There's no pleasing you, is there?" he gibed. "This morning I was a swine who wanted only to use you. Now, when I try to help you, I'm some other sort of swine."

"What are you doing down here, anyway?" she asked. She put her hands on her hips and looked at him suspiciously. In the low-ceilinged gloom of the basement, he seemed taller than ever, and the grime and sweat he had accumulated made him look more disturbingly masculine than usual. "I thought Calvin fixed everything down here yesterday."

He raised the glass, drained it in one long thirsty pull, then handed it back. He wiped his mouth with his forearm. "He couldn't possibly have fixed everything," he replied acidly. "There's too much to be done. This house should be gone over, every inch of it."

"How generous of you to volunteer."

He eyed her without amusement. "Be careful, Kimberly, or I shall 'grab' you again. Only this time my hands will leave prints." He outstretched one hand to her, opening it so that she could see the streaks of dirt.

She took another step backward.

He smiled, but again without real mirth. "Don't worry. You're safe. I won't besmirch you." He put a particularly sardonic spin on the word *besmirch*.

She turned and left him, stamping up the stairs to show her displeasure. He looked after her. Then his sharp eyes roamed over the dim and shadowy reaches of the basement. He slapped the rough wood of an overhanging beam so hard that dust showered down. "Damn!" he said about everything in general. "Damn!"

LELA MUNROE came back, her arms full of purchases. She looked askance when she saw Alec emerge from the basement, sweaty, dirty and with his shirt undone and open to the waist.

"Well," she said to Kimberly, who was fixing roast for supper, "haven't you got all the men busy as bees? But bees don't work unless they get honey, do they? Be careful, dear. Don't give it away cheap. You don't look like you can afford to."

Kimberly stared after her in outrage. Dodo would never countenance outright rudeness to a guest, but Lela Munroe made Kimberly fume with anger.

Dodo invited Alec and Calvin to eat with them. Calvin accepted happily. Alec, to Kimberly's relief, excused himself. He went upstairs to shower, and then left the house, not saying where he was going. He looked almost military in his precisely pressed khaki clothes and high boots.

Calvin ate heartily, which seemed to do Dodo's heart good. Kimberly could only pick at her food. Calvin was attentive to Dodo, but he kept one observant eye on Kimberly.

"Where's he going? The man from the Land of Auz?" he asked her.

"I don't know," Kimberly replied. "He doesn't tell me."

"Hmm," mused Calvin. "I hear he turned up at almost three in the morning at the hotel, using the phone again. Talked a long time. The night clerk told me."

Kimberly shrugged. She dissected a potato then lost interest in it.

"Maybe he's got a girl back in Australia," Calvin suggested with maddening nonchalance. "They're about sixteen time zones away. That would explain it."

Kimberly laid down her knife and fork. She was not hungry.

"Nice of him to help out around here, though," Calvin went on. "He's right. A lot to be done to keep up a house like this. He's certainly thorough. Spent this whole beautiful day in that basement. I didn't see that much to be done down there myself."

"He's just so kind," marveled Dodo, putting another slice of roast on Calvin's plate.

"He sure is," Calvin replied, his eyes locked with Kimberly's. "You know, Miss Dodo, you keep that basement really tidy. I don't know how he got himself so dirty. He must have been over every inch of it."

Kimberly looked away, feeling slightly ill. She knew what message Calvin was sending her. *Do not trust this man. Something is going on. Don't be taken in, Kimberly.*

He would say nothing aloud for fear of alarming Dodo. Kimberly stared unseeingly into the living room, where the dying evening light fell through the windows. She thought unhappily, at least Calvin's concerned about us. Somebody cares.

She turned back to look at her aunt's aging but beautiful face and suddenly wished that Dodo would return Calvin's affection. He pretended to be far more of a rascal than he was, and Dodo brought out the best in him. He would be quite a sensible and safe man to love. Not at all like some she could name.

Once more Alec did not come home until late. Kimberly was in bed and heard him. This time he was not alone. Lela Munroe was with him. From the sound of it, she'd been drinking again. Kimberly heard her furtive giggles in the hall, her, "Alec—don't! No! Don't! Oh, don't do that to me! Don't! Don't!"

They're neither one any good, Kimberly thought bitterly. She felt almost sick. She put her head under the pillow so nobody would hear her cry. She was stupid, stupid, stupid, she told herself. If they gave medals for stupidity, hers would be solid gold. The family curse was true—no Simpson woman should ever try to love.

LELA SPENT breakfast smirking so possessively at Alec that Kimberly could not watch. She escaped upstairs to strip the beds. When she pulled the sheets from Lela's, her heart almost stopped beating. This time she actually did feel ill.

Alec's khaki shirt lay tangled in Lela's sheets. Kimberly's strength came back in a rush of anger, and she snatched it up, stuffing it into the laundry basket. So Lela had finally got what she wanted. Good for her, Kimberly thought furiously. Good for Alec, too. If he was so anxious to bed a woman, he might as well get one both willing and experienced.

She made up the bed afresh. She patted everything smooth, then stood back looking at it. A fresh surge of anger overtook her, and she released it by punching the pillow as hard as she could. A feather flew up and drifted lazily in the sunlight, as if to mock her. She punched the pillow a second time, so hard she almost wrenched her arm. Then, ashamed of the childish show, she smoothed the coverlet again and went back downstairs.

Calvin had already arrived, the Fremont sisters were off to see the dinosaur park, and Lela Munroe, setting some sort of endurance record, was off shopping again. Calvin got a ladder and prepared to brave the roof and repair the shingles.

Alec, looking disgustingly innocent, seemed to be concentrating on puttering around and inspecting the first floor of the house today. Kimberly felt a fresh spurt of fiery anger every time she saw him. She avoided him so pointedly even Dodo asked her what was wrong. Kimberly said nothing at all was wrong, then disproved it by refusing to eat lunch with the others. Instead she went downtown and sat in the park, eating an ice-cream cone. Like the stupid child she was, she thought blackly.

When she returned home, she avoided him with even greater coldness. At last Alec caught her alone in the laundry room. It was almost five o'clock. He came up behind her, and when she whirled around, surprised, to face him, he almost pinned her to the wall.

"All right," he demanded between his teeth, "what's the bloody blinking matter with you now?"

"Don't you swear at me," Kimberly ordered, setting her jaw like iron.

"Then don't stick up your pretty nose at me," he retorted, "or I'll turn the bloody air blue with curses. Would you mind telling me what I've done now to offend you?"

"Oh, really," Kimberly said in distaste. "Just get out of here, will you? Go creep in a closet or climb up the chimney or whatever it is you're doing today."

He had her by the arms and he gave her a shake, a rather hard one. "Was it my fixing the hot water tap? Gluing down the loose tile? Ah! Perhaps my heinous act of unjamming the dining room window."

"Go away, you—you—" Kimberly groped for a word disgusting enough "—you *germ*."

He shook his head in furious amazement. "I don't believe this," he muttered, a dangerous edge in his voice. "You just called me a bloody germ."

"Germ," she repeated with intense satisfaction. "Microbe. Bacteria. Virus. *Mold spore*."

"Oh, you've gone too far this time, my girl," he said, nodding angrily. His eyes flashed blue fire. "Take those words back."

"I take them back, all right," she tossed at him. "It's an insult to respectable mold spores everywhere. Mold spores are an advanced life-form compared to you."

"I shall shake you insensible unless you tell me what's got into you," he threatened. "I mean it, Kimberly."

She reached into the laundry basket, snatching up the khaki shirt. She flourished it in his face. "Here," she said, then flung it against his chest. "You lost this."

He caught it but kept her trapped against the wall. "Where did you get this?" he demanded.

"Where you lost it," she snapped. "In Lela Munroe's bed. You weren't very discreet."

He gritted his teeth in impatience. He dropped the shirt and took her by both arms again. A muscle twitched in his jaw. "Kimberly, I swear to you, I found the silly cow when the hotel was closing. She'd drunk too much, and I thought I should drive her home. She was amorous, but I wasn't. As for the shirt, she nearly tore it off my back."

"Oh," said Kimberly sarcastically, "and who could blame her? You're so incredibly irresistible."

"I'm not irresistible," he said, his teeth still clenched. "You're proof of that. That woman, on the other hand, is a shark. In the hall she seized me by the shirtfront and wouldn't let go. I unbuttoned the shirt and let her have it. Me? Want Lela Munroe? By heaven, Kimberly, give me some credit."

She glared up at him, but doubt began to gnaw the edge of her anger.

"I swear," he said earnestly. He raised his right hand toward heaven. "I was as virtuous as a saint. I tried to get away, and all she'd do was hang on and say, 'Oh, Alec, don't! Don't do that to me! Don't!' She would have wrestled a lesser man to the floor and had her way with him."

He smiled at her suddenly. Somehow, she couldn't help smiling back.

He took a strand of hair and wound it gently around his finger. "So this is all quite ridiculous," he finished, his voice low.

Kimberly sighed, feeling almost hopeful again. "You're impossible." She shook her head.

"No," he corrected. "*You* are impossible. Totally. Let's make up. Kiss me."

He bent to kiss her, but she dodged slightly, eluding him. "I'm really supposed to believe that Lela Munroe only got your shirt into bed?"

"Yes. So kiss me."

Again he tried, but again she put off his attempt. His lips grazed her ear, making it burn. "Don't," she said. "Stop."

"No," he said, nuzzling her ear again. "I won't stop until I've made improper advances to you in every room of this house. Which doesn't mean, of course, that I don't respect you terribly."

"You respect nothing," she said, trying to ignore the way his mouth moved down the sensitive side of her throat.

"Come here," he commanded. He put his arms around her. "You think my intentions are dishonorable. I'll prove otherwise. To you and to the world. Look out the window."

Confused, Kimberly did so. She could see Lela Munroe coming up the front walk, shopping bags in both hands. Alec took the opportunity to push Kimberly's hair aside and give her a kiss on the nape of her neck.

"We shall also confront the incredible shopping shark," he said. "Up you go." He swept her into his arms.

"What?" Kimberly gasped, but he strode out the door and into the kitchen, holding her as if he were bearing her safely across a river. He headed for the front door. When Dodo crossed his path in the living room, she looked at them with frank astonishment. Her mouth dropped open.

"Goodness gracious," she said, then put her hand to her lips.

"Madame," Alec said, "I must tell you I find your niece attractive. I can hide it no longer."

"Goodness gracious," Dodo repeated as he carried Kimberly through the front door and onto the porch.

Lela Munroe, looking harried from an arduous day of purchasing, stopped in her tracks when Alec appeared.

Calvin, who was pounding some loose nails back into a flower planter on front of the porch, also stared.

Alec grinned at him. "Hullo, Calvin. I've come to announce to the world that I find this woman incredibly attractive. I intend to court her in due and proper fashion. I also announce that I respect her deeply and with all my heart."

Lela Munroe blinked, then blinked again, her mouth drawing down sharply. Alec addressed her. "And you, my good woman—and I used that term loosely—nearly put me in this lady's bad graces by your unwarranted assault upon my shirt."

"Well!" huffed Lela. "I never!" Hoisting her shopping bags grimly, she stalked past the two of them and into the house, slamming the door.

"True," Alec agreed, looking into Kimberly's eyes. "She never. And I never. At least not with her. Now, kiss me, Kim, out in the sun for all the world to see."

Kimberly gazed at him helplessly. She had her arms around his neck because it seemed the only logical place for them. She was conscious that Calvin still stared at them, but Calvin seemed part of another universe, one not quite real any longer.

"And you keep telling me I'm melodramatic and theatrical," she breathed, shaking her head. "What do you call this?"

"Maybe I'm just speaking your own language, love," he answered, looking into her eyes. "Or maybe at heart we're two of a kind." Before she could say otherwise, his lips captured hers.

He stood, holding her in his arms and kissing her thoroughly, as the warm afternoon sun spilled down its gold. The scent of roses rode the balmy wind.

"This is crazy," Kimberly said against his lips when he drew back briefly.

"Mad. Quite mad," he agreed and kissed her again. Somewhere a bluebird sang.

CHAPTER SEVEN

"IT's NOT that I object to your being interested in Kimberly," Dodo said weakly. She sat at the kitchen table, her head between her hands. Her elbows were propped inelegantly on the table, and she seemed to be staring at some specter that nobody else could see. "I just—" she continued, then swallowed hard. "I just don't think one ought to be so...demonstrative in public—right in broad daylight."

"What she's saying," Calvin muttered dryly, "is you don't have to make a spectacle of yourselves." He stood behind Dodo, his arms crossed sternly.

Kimberly, also seated at the table, felt her face growing hot. She supposed it had been a spectacle—Alec carrying her through the house, announcing to the world that he intended to court her in "due and proper" fashion, then kissing her right there on the front porch in the afternoon sunlight.

"Sorry," Alec said, clearly unrepentant. He picked up the teapot and poured Dodo a cup, which he set before her. "Kimberly refused to believe me unless I stated my case as strongly as possible. Desperate problems require desperate remedies."

"Mrs. Munroe checked out," Calvin accused, still the stern guardian. "She was offended. Miss Dodo makes her living by taking in guests. You two needn't drive them off with your Romeo and Juliet act."

Kimberly sank more deeply and guiltily into her chair.

"I don't regret Mrs. Munroe's leaving," Dodo protested feebly. She took a sip of tea, as if to strengthen herself. "She'd already stayed two days longer than she'd originally planned. And I must say I've heard her come in the past two nights, well, in a rather unfortunate way."

"Precisely," Alec agreed. "And her rather unfortunate ways made Kimberly doubt me. I'm sorry to have embarrassed you, Miss Simpson. I shall conduct myself more conventionally from now on."

Kimberly stole a look at her aunt. So Dodo had heard Lela Munroe's late night entrances, too. She must have also heard her breathy giggling advance to Alec the night before. Dodo's ears had always been preternaturally sharp.

Dodo took another sip of tea. She looked harried. "The question is not whether Mrs. Munroe is a lady," she said, giving Alec a disturbed look. "The point is I tried to raise Kimberly to be one."

"I understand, ma'am," Alec murmured. "I'll treat her so—I promise you."

"See that you do," growled Calvin.

"I'd like to take Kimberly to supper tonight," Alec said, apparently still unfazed. "She hasn't really been out since she came home. I'll have her in early because I have some business down in Fayetteville."

Dodo looked first at her niece, who knew she still looked guilty, then at Alec Shaughnessy, who smiled as if he had never learned the meaning of the word *guilt*. "Surely you're not asking my permission, Mr. Shaughnessy," Dodo replied, shaking her head. "Kimberly's an adult. She's free to do as she wishes. I'm only concerned about the two of you having a—a relationship while you stay in this house."

"Would you have rather I'd kept my attentions secret, Miss Simpson?" Alec asked, one brow cocking critically. "I decided it was time to be open. You do believe honesty is the best policy?''

"Of course," Dodo began. "But I—"

Alec cut her off smoothly. "I swear I'll make no improper advance toward Kimberly while I'm a guest in this house. I will guard her virtue and her reputation like jewels. I give my solemn vow."

Kimberly's head swam. It seemed that Alec had already made quite a number of improper advances toward her, as well as some extremely effective assaults on her virtue. Now he and her aunt were talking about her as if she weren't even there. And somehow Calvin, who should have nothing to do with it at all, was scowling at her as if he were actually her protective uncle.

Dodo, however, showed surprising resiliency, in spite of her disturbance. "It's for Kimberly to say if she wants to go out with you, not me," she stated, shaking her head. "And if you vow to be a gentleman, then it's your own conscience you must answer to, not me. But I am not a woman who gives or takes a vow lightly, Mr. Shaughnessy. Nor, do I think, is Kimberly."

"Me, neither," added Calvin, warning in his voice.

Alec walked around the table. He thrust his hand out to Calvin. "I said I swear it, and I do. I give my word to you as well."

Calvin paused a moment. He studied Alec's outstretched hand, then glanced at Dodo. "See that you keep it, Shaughnessy," he said and looked Alec in the eye.

Alec met his gaze calmly, shook hands, then turned to Kimberly. "Well," he said, fixing his intent blue gaze on her. "Will you? Come with me tonight?"

Again Kimberly felt slightly dizzied by events. "Yes," she said, looking at the apprehension on Dodo's face. "I suppose."

"I'll go shower and change," he said. He turned and left the kitchen. When he was gone, Calvin finally sat down at the table. He gave Kimberly a hopeless look.

"Kimberly—" he began, but Dodo held up her hand, signaling him to stop.

"This was bound to happen," Dodo said with resignation. "A girl as special as Kimberly—some male guest was bound to notice her sooner or later. Perhaps it's best it happened now. And with Mr. Shaughnessy, who at least is a gentleman and has shown us nothing but goodness."

"Dodo," Calvin said earnestly, "are you actually going to let him stay here? You don't know if you can trust him."

"It was bound to happen," Dodo repeated doggedly. "I'll have to follow my instincts. I believe I can trust him. And, Calvin, I *know* I can trust Kimberly. That's what's important."

Calvin gave Kimberly a look that told her she'd better be trustworthy or she would be in exceptionally deep trouble with him. "Yes. Being able to trust Kimberly. That's what's important."

Dodo smiled at last, a tired but loving smile. She reached over and patted Kimberly's hand. "My girl won't fail me. Will you, dear? She never has."

Kimberly seized hold of Dodo's hand and squeezed it hard. Dodo squeezed back. "Oh, goodness," she said, glancing up at the kitchen clock. "It's time to put on the lamb stew. I expect it will be just the two of us this evening, Calvin, what with the young people going out."

"I expect it will, ma'am," Calvin answered. In spite of the day's events, Kimberly saw that the prospect of being alone with Dodo made a deeply pleased look creep over his weathered face.

KIMBERLY DRESSED in her best summer dress, a pale pink cotton with a halter top and a full, embroidered eyelet skirt. Alec, in white slacks and short-sleeved shirt, seemed almost to glow in the hazy early-evening light. He had selected a German restaurant out at the edge of town, and they drove there in his rented convertible.

Alec tossed her a wry glance as he wheeled the car along the winding road. "Do you have the feeling that things between us are so topsy-turvy we've begun to live backward?"

"What do you mean?" Kimberly asked. She had tied her hair back so it wouldn't blow in the open car. She fiddled with the pink ribbon self-consciously.

"I mean," he answered, his mouth crooking, "that yesterday I held you half naked in my arms, and now we're going out on our first date, which seems distinctly backward."

She looked away, watching the dark crowd of pines that lined the road.

"Worse," he said, mockery in his voice, "you've forced me to tell the world, including your aunt, how intriguing I find you. Worst, I've promised to behave. Instead of trying to get you into my bed, where you would be delicious, I've pledged my honor on keeping you out of it—obviously the move of a madman."

She shrugged uncomfortably. He turned the car into the parking lot of the long, rustic-looking building that housed the restaurant. He took the key out of the ignition, toyed with it, but didn't get out. "Do you know why I did it?" he asked.

His gaze roamed over her face, fell to the swell of her breasts, then came back to her face. She felt slightly breathless, as if something momentous was going to happen. "Why you did what?" she asked.

"Why I made all those blasted solemn vows about your honor and mine?" he asked. He reached his hand along the back of the seat as if to trace his forefinger against the curve of her cheek. He barely touched her, then drew his hand back.

She could only watch him. He clenched his hand into a fist, set it on the dashboard. He regarded it, then her with unhappy resignation. "I had to swear not to touch you," he said, his low voice harsh. "At least not touch you in all the ways I want. For unless I pledge my last ounce of honor, I won't be able to resist making love to you."

Kimberly tossed her head nervously. "Don't be presumptuous. What makes you think I'd let you?"

Fire flashed deep within his gaze. "Because when we touch, the rest of the world goes away, and nothing matters but the two of us. Men have died for feeling so. And women have been lost. Maybe I want to spare you. Or simply spare myself."

Kimberly's emotions tumbled into even more dangerous disorder. She looked up at the sky. She made a helpless gesture with her hands. "What's happening to us?" she asked, almost pleading. For something extraordinary was happening between her and Alec, something that seemed both wonderful and terrifying.

"I don't know," he answered grimly. "All I can do is make a promise to you, Kimberly. That I will never hurt you if I can help it."

THE RESTAURANT was a pleasant and prospering one, casual rather than elegant, more homey than high-toned. But, as usually happened to things when Alec was around, it became slightly unreal to Kimberly, a bit dreamlike.

It seemed to her, as soon as they entered the restaurant, that they began, by silent agreement, to play a long charade. They chatted amiably enough of ordinary things, the way any couple might when they were becoming better acquainted.

Beneath their conversation, though, a stronger, wordless conversation ran. The emotion it carried was stronger than anything else in the room. Electricity seemed to pulse between them, quiet, but ready to surge into earth-shaking power. They pretended to be engrossed in ordinary things, eating, drinking, and talking.

Kimberly had the roasted duck, but as delicious as she knew it was, she felt she might as well have dined on clouds. The wine could have been imaginary, for all she knew—an illusion created by a spell.

"Calvin is completely taken with your aunt, you know." Alec smiled, regarding her over the rim of his wineglass. "Will she ever reciprocate?"

"I don't know." She toyed with a cherry from her Black Forest cake. "I'm not sure Calvin would ever be bold enough to propose. I think beneath all the eccentricity, he's really shy. I'd never suspected."

"Dodo is still beautiful," Alec observed. "I'm surprised she wasn't carried off by some suitor long ago."

"Oh," Kimberly said, spearing the cherry neatly. "That couldn't happen while my grandfather was around. He thought his descendents existed for his sake only. If anyone dared look at Dodo, I'm sure the colonel scared him off. He was very good at scaring people."

"What about you?" Alec smiled. "Did he keep you to himself, too?"

"He tried," Kimberly admitted. "But I was rebellious. And to tell the truth, I don't think he liked me much. I was the symbol that somebody had dared to defy him. My mother. She just didn't do it very well."

"And your aunt—she never rebelled?"

"Dodo lives to please others," Kimberly stated. "It's how she can cope with the innkeeping business. I feel guilty now—my grandfather died, and I just went off to live my own life. I didn't worry about Dodo—even after all she'd done for me."

He examined her face soberly. "Dodo wouldn't want you to worry. She seemed to want you to have what she didn't. A free and independent existence."

Kimberly nodded, a lump of regret in her throat. "But I just ... went off. Not caring for anybody in the world but myself. I left for Kansas City, thinking I was going to be an artist. What a joke."

"Kimberly," Alec told her, "don't be so hard on yourself. You were very young then, and the young are supposed to be selfish. Nature makes them so, and for a reason—so they can break free."

"But I didn't break free," she protested softly. "I came home again."

"Not quite as young and not nearly so selfish, I'll warrant. As for art, you've approached that the way you approach everything. Courageously—but impatiently. Did it never occur to you that such things take time?"

"Time?" she asked, then fell silent as the waiter approached and lit the candle on their table. Outside, through the big picture windows, she could see night falling on the mountains.

"Time," he repeated, watching the candlelight gild the curve of her cheek. "How much formal art training have you had?"

"None," she replied ruefully. "I thought I had talent and that I'd make it. I was wrong."

"You were wrong," he said, "only about how quickly you might make it. Surely you didn't expect it to happen overnight. The talent's there. It needs direction, that's all. And time.''

Kimberly felt warmed by his praise, but not quite believing. ''That's nice of you to say,'' she answered, ''but it may not be true.''

He regarded her with bemusement. ''I know a bit about art. About composition. In fact, I'd say that's your strength—an unusually good eye for composition. I'd be willing to bet that when the ad agency hired you, you did some storyboarding for them, eh?''

Kimberly nodded, surprised. A storyboard artist worked with a director, designing the shots that would be used in a piece of video tape or film. She could storyboard like a very demon. It was in the details, finding the precise image that Mr. Mussfarber wanted for his mustard that she had failed.

''I'm right,'' Alec asserted, appraising her expression correctly. ''Give yourself some time and study, my girl. You'll make an artist yet. I'll drink to it.''

He drained his glass. The waiter came to refill it, but Alec requested coffee instead. ''I've got to drive to Fayetteville yet,'' he said. ''I don't intend to maneuver these coiling roads with too much wine in me.''

''Fayetteville, tonight?'' Kimberly asked. ''These roads are treacherous at night, Alec—really. Do you have to?''

''Sorry,'' he murmured, ''I have an appointment.'' He examined her questioning face, then added, ''Folklorist. Retired professor from the university. Strange old boy. Sleeps all day, prefers to work at night. Fewer interruptions, he says.''

''You know,'' Kimberly said, smiling somewhat shamefacedly, ''I don't even know what you're going to do with all this information. Write a book? Are you a professor yourself?''

He stirred sugar into his coffee. "Yes, actually. In Brisbane. I was thinking along the lines of a book. Or a television documentary, perhaps. On superstition. These hills are rich in stories, you know."

She nodded. Too many stories, she thought, remembering the ones that had circulated about her house and family.

He reached for her hand. He held it, looking down at it in the candlelight. His clasp was careful, almost clinical. But even that impartial and unemotional touch set Kimberly's pulses beating hard. She wondered if he could feel them.

If he did, he gave no indication. "There's a rhyme, for instance," he said thoughtfully. "A way to tell the immediate future. One simply counts the white spots on a person's fingernails." He spread her fingers slightly, then, using the forefinger on his other hand, traced her nails, rhyming,

"A gift, a ghost, a friend, a foe;
A letter to come, a journey to go."

He released her hand. She flexed her fingers, regarding them in the flickering light. "All that?" she asked, not wanting to look at him. "A gift, a ghost, a friend—" she could not finish the rest.

"A foe," he supplied, his voice suddenly cool. "A letter to come. A journey to go. Right now I've a journey to go myself. I'll take you home. Early, as I promised."

They spoke no more as he paid the bill and walked her to the car. "A bit of a chill," he said at last, going to the driver's side. "Here. Take my jacket."

"It's all right—" Kimberly started to protest, but he was already reaching into the backseat. She turned and looked down. In the bluish haze of the parking lot lights, she saw him lift the khaki jacket. Beneath it was the box she had found in the drawer of his room, the box from India with Ganesha on its lid.

Smoothly he slid the box beneath a pile of books and magazines so that it was hidden again. He handed Kimberly the jacket. She draped it uneasily around her shoulders.

"That box," she said, glancing at his implacable profile in the half-light. "With Ganesha on it . . ."

He didn't even bother to glance at her. "That? Nothing. Something I picked up in town. Yesterday."

Kimberly looked away, biting her lip. He pulled out of the parking lot and onto the winding darkness of the road.

Perhaps it meant nothing, she thought uncomfortably. Perhaps he hadn't meant to keep the box hidden, and she had merely misinterpreted his move. But if he'd bought the box in Eureka, he had done so before yesterday. She had seen it earlier in the week. Why would he lie? Or had he simply forgotten, made an unimportant mistake?

He pulled the car up to the house. Kimberly could see Dodo sitting on the porch. "Don't bother walking me to the door," Kimberly said, slipping out of Alec's jacket and handing it to him. Then, before he could protest, she opened the door and stepped out. She turned to face him, her pink skirt whirling slightly. "Thank you for supper," she said. "It was delicious."

He looked at her a long moment. The dim golden glow of the street lamp fell on both of them. "Your company is what was delicious," he said at last. He smiled slightly. "And I meant what I said. I'll never hurt you if I can help it, Kimberly. If I could give you any gift in the world, that would be it. And you can give me a gift in return."

"Yes?" She stood, looking at him expectantly.

"Keep your door locked at night," he said, the cool smile never wavering. "It's a great temptation for me to lie in bed thinking it might be open. Make sure it never is. Goodnight, love."

He put the car back into gear, and Kimberly, embarrassed by the emotions that flared warmly through her, turned and fled to the porch and Dodo's comforting presence. Behind her, she heard the Thunderbird convertible pull away.

She bent and kissed Dodo on the cheek, then sank into the cushions of the porch swing, feeling drained and somehow exhausted. Without a doubt, Alec Shaughnessy was the most maddening and contradictory human being she had ever met.

"Did you have a pleasant time, dear?" Dodo asked. "Mr. Shaughnessy got you home early, just as he said. I'm glad. Although I wasn't really worried."

"Everything was nice," Kimberly said evasively. Every time she encountered Alec, it seemed, she had to spend the next half dozen hours sorting out her thoughts and feelings about him. "What about you?" she asked, gently turning the tables.

"Oh, my," Dodo said in exasperation. "Do you know that I let myself get so confused over you and Mr. Shaughnessy that I didn't realize I was left alone, entertaining a gentleman—all by myself? What will people think?"

Kimberly curled up comfortably in the swing, letting its soft motion lull her. "Dodo," she replied, "nobody would ever think anything bad of you. Besides, I'm sure the Fremont sisters were along before the evening was over, so you weren't really alone."

"I know," sighed Dodo, "I shouldn't worry." She sat for a long moment, staring at the play of the street lamp's glow on the leaves. "But what really bothers me," she added at last, "is that I didn't even think about it until dessert time. It seemed so... natural to have him there. That sounds impossible, doesn't it—that I got so used so quickly to having him around?"

Kimberly smiled in the darkness and was glad her aunt couldn't see. "Calvin's an extremely nice man," she said. "He never puts on airs and he fits right in. I've gotten used to having him around myself."

"You have?" The relief in Dodo's voice was evident.

"Really," Kimberly assured her. "I imagine if he suddenly stopped coming around, I'd miss him."

"You would? Honestly, Kimberly? It's odd, isn't it? I mean he's so different from us."

It was Kimberly's turn to sigh. She leaned back against the cushions and watched the moths dance out their nightly obsession around the streetlight. "He's not so different, Dodo," she said softly. "He's always been a little bit of an outsider in town, just like us. And I suppose, like us, he's a little lonely."

Dodo thought for a moment. "Why," she said softly, "it never occurred to me to look at it that way. You know, in a way, Calvin is even like Father, like the colonel. In that he's an individualist, I mean. He's gone his own way through life. That takes a great deal of courage."

"Dodo," Kimberly said firmly, "Calvin's *unlike* Grandfather in every other way—that's what I like about him. The colonel wasn't exactly the easiest person in the world to get along with—even for you."

"Oh, goodness no," Dodo admitted. "But you see, he needed someone so badly—"

"The colonel?" Kimberly suppressed a laugh of disbelief. "The colonel never needed anybody—except to dominate."

"It wasn't like that," Dodo contradicted softly. "He just seemed to depend on us so much, especially after Mother—left us. She died within a year after we came home from India. She never even saw this house completed. We were living at the hotel then . . . and the colonel was bereft."

Kimberly turned the idea over in her mind. It seemed strange—the colonel being bereft over anyone or anything. Her grandmother was a shadowy figure to her, far dimmer than even her mother. For some reason, there were not even any pictures of her in the house. "Did they really love each other that much?" Kimberly had difficulty imagining the colonel feeling tender toward anyone.

Dodo was silent a long moment. The tree frogs sang and the crickets whirred. "I think he loved her that much—in his way," she said. "But she stopped loving him. That's what made it so sad. One of the reasons I always felt he was so—in need."

Kimberly sat up straight. She stared through the shadows at Dodo. "She stopped loving him? Dodo, you never told me that. I always assumed Grandmother fit right into the mold—her world revolved around the colonel. You mean it didn't?"

"It never seemed to me," Dodo said uncomfortably, "a story that should burden a child. And I'm not sure I understood what happened myself. Your mother knew more than I did, I think. She was closer to Mother than I was. Mother just began to drift away from the colonel in India. And from me, too, for some reason."

Kimberly cocked her head in curiosity. "Your own mother turned away from you?" she asked in disbelief.

"Yes, dear," Dodo replied calmly. "Such things happen. The human heart is very complicated. Which is why I worry about you. I didn't mean to take on so today when I saw you in Mr. Shaughnessy's arms, but it was so unconventional—and I must admit, Kimberly, it was like seeing something I'd always imagined come true—almost too true."

Kimberly stayed tensed against the cushions, staring at her aunt's diminutive figure in the darkness. "What do you mean, come true?" she asked.

"It's silly, I know," Dodo said worriedly, "but ever since you were small, I had to prepare for the day you'd leave this house and I wouldn't have you anymore. And I hoped that you'd have a better life—a fuller life than your mother and I did. That things would be more . . . normal for you. And so I always imagined you going away with a man. Not slipping away to meet him secretly and running off some night, the way your mother did. Somehow I always imagined he would come for you and take you where you belonged. Actually bear you away in his arms in broad daylight. And you would go with him proudly, your arms around his neck. So you can imagine my shock when I saw just that—I know, I know—you'll think I've read too many novels or poems. But you both had such a look on your faces . . ."

Her voice trailed off. Kimberly felt suddenly wary and confused again. "What kind of look?"

"Just a look," Dodo said. "A kind of shining. The sort of look I imagine people in love have."

Kimberly swallowed hard. "Mr. Shaughnessy and I aren't in love."

There was a heartbeat of silence. "Aren't you, dear?" Dodo asked gently. Kimberly shook her head in negation, but she could not bring herself to say No. The two of them were quiet again.

"You're not afraid of that silly curse, are you?" Dodo asked softly.

Kimberly's throat felt tight. These last few days, she actually had been afraid.

"Pay it no attention," Dodo counseled. She almost laughed. "You know, your mother always claimed the colonel made the whole thing up. Just to keep us in line. Who knows—he may have.''

"Made it up?" Kimberly asked, horrified. "But that would be horrible! Why would he do such a thing?"

"I don't know that he did," Dodo replied with a shrug. "But I do know that he was afraid of losing any more. He was a man who lost too much in his time."

"What?" asked Kimberly. She had always thought of the colonel as a man who had managed to keep everything to himself.

"So much," Dodo repeated. "India. The place he loved. The rajah—the friend he loved. Finally, my mother—the woman he loved. Sometimes I think it wasn't we who were cursed but that jewel. India is full of cursed jewels, you know."

"The Heart of the Sun?" Kimberly asked.

"The topaz, yes," Dodo replied. "Everything seemed to go wrong after it came into the rajah's hands. It destroyed him. It destroyed Sir Cyril Damon. And ultimately did the colonel nothing but ill. I've often wondered what happened to it. Cut into a hundred smaller stones I suppose. And scattered around the world. It let Sir Cyril survive, I suppose, heaven help his soul."

The two women lapsed into silence. At last Dodo rose and came to the swing. She kissed Kimberly on the forehead. "I have to go to bed, dear. It's been a long day and a strange one. That means I'll dream of India tonight—it always happens. Good night. And don't stay up too late."

Kimberly caught up her aunt's hand and give it an affectionate squeeze. "Good night," she said.

She sat up late, rocking in the swing, staring out into the peaceful night.

She gazed up at the dark sky. Some people said one could foretell the future from the stars, and Kimberly wished she could. She thought of Alec, and the familiar shudder of pleasure and sweet dread shook her clear through. She remembered his fingers touching hers so carefully in the restaurant, and she counted his predictions again:

"A gift, a ghost, a friend, a foe,
A letter to come, a journey to go."

He had said he would give her a gift—that he would never hurt her if he could help it. But that was only one small part of the prophecy. Who was the ghost? Who the friend and who the foe? What letter would come for her? What journey must she take?

The stars gave no reply.

CHAPTER EIGHT

THE LIGHT sparkled like gold dust the next morning, giving the leaves and grass a rich glow. In the distance the mountains looked like jade-covered velvet.

When Kimberly and Alec met at the breakfast table, they smiled. The smile made her feel as if something magical drew them together, separating them from the everyday world. But their greetings were ordinary and polite, for Dodo and the Fremont sisters were at the table as well.

Kimberly was concerned because Alec, who normally radiated vitality, looked weary. His gaze, when not on her, seemed distracted, almost haggard. The lines that fanned out from his eyes were more deeply engraved than usual. The set of his mouth was both defiant and cynical.

"Did you have a pleasant trip to Fayetteville?" Dodo asked him as she poured his coffee. "It was productive, I hope?"

"Yes," he said vaguely.

"You look tired," Dodo said, sitting down. "I hope you slept all right. I swear I heard something in the attic again last night. But that's impossible."

Alec looked at her sharply. "Indeed? I'll check. You do have sharp ears, Miss Simpson."

"My father always said that Nature was compensating for my dim sight," Dodo laughed. "But at two in the morning, I'd just as soon not hear quite as well."

"Yes," Alec said. "Well. I'll check the attic one last time. I'll be inspecting the upstairs anyway."

"You needn't check anything," Dodo protested. "You've done too much for us already."

"Nonsense," Alec said. "I enjoy it." But his expression was troubled. He glanced at Kimberly and gave her the ghost of a smile. Then he lapsed into his own thoughts, and his face grew clouded once more.

After breakfast the Fremont sisters left to visit a friend at Holiday Island. Alec lingered over his coffee. Kimberly started to clear the rest of the table, but Dodo stopped her. "No more work today," she said with surprising firmness. "You've forgotten what day it is, haven't you?"

Kimberly looked at her aunt first with puzzlement, then pleasure. Alec cocked a bronze eyebrow. "A special day, is it?"

"It's her twenty-first birthday," Dodo replied proudly. "We'll have a special lunch to celebrate. In the meantime, no more chores. Take the day to work on your art, Kimberly."

"I shall have to buy you a proper gift," Alec said, rising from his chair. "And take you out tonight. That is, if your aunt hasn't made other plans."

"Kimberly's evening should be special," Dodo replied. "And it's kind of you to offer to make it so."

"Kimberly?" he asked, smiling slightly.

"I'd love to," she answered shyly. She was conscious that Dodo watched them closely. Her face clearly said, "Aha! There's something between these two, all right."

Kimberly gave Alec a last smile and excused herself. Taking her sketch book, she took sanctuary in the garden. After breakfast, Calvin arrived, and Kimberly, from her lawn chair, could hear him clanking and pounding in the kitchen, trying to intimidate the garbage disposal back into obedience. Alec took a break at ten-thirty and came out to the garden.

Once more his jeans were dusty, his shirt streaked with sweat and grime. Where, she wondered, could he possibly be working? Dodo kept the second floor as neat as the proverbial pin. He must be getting into nooks and spots no one had troubled with for years.

He gave her a tired grin, but the glance that roamed over her white shorts and blouse was appreciative. He threw himself down in the grass beside her lawn chair, leaning his head back so that his hair just brushed her bare thigh. He reached up and took her hand. "Your grandfather didn't build a house," he said, kissing her knuckles. "He built a bloody Chinese puzzle. Even the corners have corners. There are window seats that open up and closets within closets. What was the old boy expecting? A revolution in which he'd hide the refugees?"

She ran her fingers over the gilded hair that fell over his forehead. "Who knows?" she asked languidly. "He liked to puzzle and confound people. But it was a wonderful house for a child to play in. And hide. Whenever the colonel was mad, I had twenty places to disappear. It'd take him forever to find me. It was wonderful."

He kissed her hand again. His face was serious, distracted. "I doubt if it was wonderful, having to escape the old boy. Had a temper, did he?"

"The devil's own," Kimberly said, then stretched in satisfaction. The colonel's tempers seemed a matter of ancient history now.

Alec kissed her palm. "And why do you suppose he wanted to confound people?" he asked. He sat up straight, still holding her hand, his expression suddenly intent.

"It was his nature," Kimberly explained. "Besides, the rajah gave him a lot of valuable gifts. A few of those hiding places were for safekeeping. I didn't know about some of them for years. The false door in the back of his closet, for instance."

"Gifts?" Alec said, lifting an inquisitive brow. "And you knew all the hiding places?"

She smiled at the memory. "Yes. Usually after the gifts were sold. Grandfather kept speculating—in mines, I think. I think he thought his investments would make him rich. That we'd entertain royally someday. But they made him poor, or nearly. So all that was left was an oversize house with a lot of peculiar cubby holes. Don't tell me you've found them all, or I'll think you're looking for something."

"I am," he said with elaborate casualness. He turned once more and leaned his head against her tanned thigh. "I'm looking for soft spots and rotten places. Give a wall a thump and think, blast! What's this? Have the ruddy termites been tunneling away? Rain damage? Dry rot? But it's only another niche or nook or closet."

"And every one empty," Kimberly smiled.

He stared up at the sky pessimistically. "Empty. Except for spider nurseries and dust memorials. How did you know?"

"I've looked," she laughed. "Those were my childhood haunts, after all. But it wouldn't be like the colonel to hide anything tremendously valuable. He only hid the lesser things."

He was silent a long moment, staring up at the flawless sky. "What do you mean?" he asked quietly.

She shrugged, studying the unusual moodiness of his handsome face. She resisted an impulse to trace the outline of his mustache. "The rajah gave him many small treasures. But a few really valuable ones. There were some rubies once." She laughed. "He didn't hide them. Do you know where he kept them? In the fishbowl. With the gold-fish swimming right over them. As if they were marbles or just decorative stones."

"The fishbowl," Alec practically groaned. "Was he totally crazy?"

"Like a fox," mused Kimberly, and gave in to the temptation to trail her forefinger along his upper lip. "Hide what's really valuable out in the open, that's what he said. What thief would look at the stones in the bottom of a fishbowl? And when the colonel needed a lot of money, he just stuck his hand in with the fish and pulled out another ruby. There were twelve, I think. He used them all. On his everlasting mines. I wish he'd left at least one for Dodo."

Alec released her hand. He stared at the big house looming up in the sunlight. "Hid his greatest treasures in the open, did he? A fox indeed. People say there still is treasure concealed here, you know. Calvin told me."

"People have said it for years," Kimberly said wryly. "People say a lot of things. If it's there, it's fooled everyone so far."

He stood. He drew her to her feet. "I'd like to put my arms around you," he said, his voice low. "But I'm a walking cobweb, a poor knight indeed, with only a cloak of dust."

He held her hands and stared down into her eyes. Once again his face held that oddly haunted look, as if he were dogged by furies he alone understood. He made Kimberly yearn to be in his arms, leaning against him, dust and all.

"Where would you want to go tonight?" he asked, lacing his fingers through hers. The question was warm, but his face was still unnaturally serious.

"Anywhere," she answered, smiling up at him. "As long as it's with you."

He looked down at her, smiling crookedly. "That's the boldest thing you've ever said to me. Turning twenty-one has made you bloom, I think."

He stared at the tall old house, and his smile faded. "I should check the outside," he muttered. "For cracks in the mortar and such. How many rocks do you suppose are in this great folly of a house?"

"I don't know," she answered, puzzled by the persistence of his brooding. "Thousands, I suppose."

He held her hands more tightly, but his eyes stayed on the house. He measured it as if it were his implacable enemy.

"Thousands," he muttered, the corners of his mouth turning down. He studied the exterior, strange stone laid upon strange stone. No two were alike. How long would it take a man to examine that great, mad mosaic of stones? Especially if he were not sure precisely what he was looking for? "Thousands," he repeated. He looked down at her.

Kimberly was puzzled by the expression darkening his eyes. It was like anger or sorrow or both.

She must be imagining it, she thought, as a breeze sprang up and rippled in the roses. The sun poured down its golden warmth, and she and Alec were together, at a new and tender stage in their relationship. Who could feel sorrow on a day like this?

CALVIN, KIMBERLY and Alec sat at the dining room table as Dodo bore in an elaborate layer cake. It was Kimberly's favorite kind, dark double chocolate with creamy white frosting. It had twenty-one white candles, all blazing.

Calvin led the singing of "Happy Birthday," then teased Kimberly to blow out the candles. He claimed the blaze of so much light was blinding him.

She stood and, pushing her hair back over her shoulders, bent and started to blow out the flames. Then she paused. She should make a wish first? Wasn't that the superstition?

She caught the glint of amusement in Alec's eyes as he leaned back in his chair, watching her. She knew what she wished for, in her heart. But then she saw Dodo's face shining in happiness for her, and Calvin secretly admiring Dodo, and she knew what her wish should be.

Happiness for Dodo, she thought fervently, and for Calvin, too. Then she inhaled deeply and blew until the last candle flickered out.

"With lungs like that you should have been an opera singer," joked Calvin. "I'm surprised you didn't blow frosting all over the wall."

"I'm surprised she didn't blow it into the next county," Alec said.

Kimberly started to make a rejoinder, but Dodo laid a finger on her lips. "Now, Mr. Shaughnessy, you study superstitions. You know that Kimberly mustn't talk before she has her first bite of cake, or else her wish won't come true."

Kimberly contented herself with wrinkling her nose derisively at Calvin and Alec, then cut into the cake and carefully laid a large slice on each plate.

Hurriedly she sat down and ate her first bite.

"And what did you wish for?" Calvin asked. "For every day to be your birthday, so you could sit in the garden and have cake for lunch?"

"She wished a spell on us," Alec offered, "that we always remain her devoted slaves."

"She can't tell her wish, or it won't come true," scolded Dodo.

"I wished for better manners for the two of you," Kimberly told the men pertly, and Dodo laughed and said, "So there!"

I wonder, thought Kimberly, almost giddy with happiness, if this will be the best birthday of my life? She was surrounded by the people of whom she was most fond—Dodo, Calvin and Alec. How quickly Calvin had come to belong with them, a part of the family. And how swiftly and deeply she had come to love Alec.

She stopped, her silver fork cutting only halfway through the cake. The word she had used so naturally in her thoughts startled her. *Love,* she thought in confusion. A week ago she would have thought it impossible.

"I have a present for you," Dodo said, reaching into her apron pocket. "It's just something sentimental, really. But I wanted you to have it for this birthday." She handed Kimberly a small box wrapped in gold foil and ornamented with a pink and gold bow.

"A present." Kimberly smiled, starting to unwrap it. "You're spoiling me hopelessly, Dodo."

Carefully she set the bow aside and took the paper from the box. She opened the lid, then gasped. "Dodo!" she whispered. "It's your brooch."

Lying in a nest of cotton was a crescent of gold encrusted with small turquoises and seed pearls. "Oh, Dodo," Kimberly said in awe, lifting the delicate piece up to examine it for the first time in years. Its back was elaborately enameled. "I thought the colonel sold this ages ago."

"He wanted to, but I wouldn't let him," Dodo answered. "I said, 'That brooch is for Kimberly, for her twenty-first birthday.'"

Kimberly gave her aunt a look of love and gratitude. The older she grew, the more she appreciated Dodo's unexpected strengths. How many times, she wondered, had her aunt stood up to the colonel on her behalf?

"The brooch is not terribly valuable," Dodo explained shyly. "But the rajah himself gave it to me on my thirteenth birthday. It symbolizes the forces of life and creation."

"I thought it was long gone," Kimberly said in wonder and fastened it to the front of her white blouse.

"I know." Dodo smiled. "I kept it out of sight so it would be a better surprise."

"I love it," Kimberly said and, rising, went to kiss her aunt on the cheek. "And I love you for saving it for me."

"Oh, it's nothing." Dodo fluttered her hands, embarrassed. "Just a curiosity, really."

Calvin cleared his throat. "I have a little something for you myself," he said gruffly. He handed her another small box, wrapped in brown paper.

"Calvin," she said, trying to sound stern, "you shouldn't have."

She sat down and removed the wrappings, revealing a battered little velvet box. Kimberly opened it and smiled in pleased disbelief. It was a pair of antique earrings made of wrought gold wire. Each piece was a small elaborate initial "K" in a frame of matching gold.

"Calvin," she said, her voice soft, "they're lovely. I've never seen anything like them."

"They were my mother's," Calvin muttered. "Her name was Kristina. I can't wear 'em, so you might as well." He gave Dodo a shy glance. "Have her wedding ring, too," he said in an almost inaudible voice.

Dodo smiled nervously.

"I love them, Calvin," Kimberly said quickly, putting the earrings on. "I'll take care of them forever. And always think of you when I wear them."

"Harrumph," harrumphed Calvin, clearly uncomfortable with all this emotion. Kimberly rose again, and before he could protest, quickly bent and kissed him on his gleaming bald head. "Harrumph," said Calvin again.

Alec watched Kimberly's shy and happy face with disconcerting intentness. "I doubt I could find you gifts finer than these. Not if I roamed the earth for a dozen years. And looked in all its rich and secret places. But I'll bring you some poor thing."

She looked at him and smiled. He smiled back. She felt herself becoming lost in the mysterious blue depths of his eyes. Suddenly aware that Dodo and Calvin were watching them, she turned away. But she understood now what Dodo had meant. She and Alec looked at each other like people in love.

THE AFTERNOON SUN was so hot and bright that Kimberly withdrew to the coolness of the living room and curled up on the love seat, sketching. She was experimenting with a complicated design involving hummingbirds and hearts.

Alec had left the house at about three and returned close to five. "Hullo," he said as he came in. "I feel practically delinquent. There are still two door knobs, three hinges and five window catches to be mended upstairs."

"Dodo will have to have you flogged," teased Kimberly. She marveled at how simply seeing him made her feel as if she were glowing all over. She could not keep from smiling at him.

He didn't smile back. He leaned against the fireplace instead. "You shouldn't smile like that," he warned quietly. "It makes you too beautiful. It takes all my willpower to keep from taking you in my arms and—well, it takes all my willpower."

Kimberly looked away.

His voice was low again. "I wonder, when I'm old, if I'll curse this moment. And think, there you were, all in white, like a fresh white rose, your long hair shimmering down. And I stood, like a fool, and only looked at you."

"You shouldn't say such things," she breathed, still not looking at him. She didn't dare. He had made her feel desirous and shuddery, both inside and out.

"I can't even make love to you with words?" he asked huskily. "You're right. Words might lead to actions. Yet I can look. You are like a rose in white, you know. If I could paint, I'd do your portrait as you are now—*Kimberly on her Twenty-First Birthday*, with the sunlight in the glory of that hair."

She shook her head self-consciously. She stole a glimpse at him. He lounged against the fireplace, tall and lean and booted. His pale blue shirt made him look more tanned and blond than usual.

"Perhaps," he smiled, "we should switch to a more neutral subject. Such as dinner or the weather or cabbages and kings. Will the Paradise restaurant be all right for dinner? It's new, but I hear it's good."

"The Paradise will be wonderful," she answered.

"Will you wear white for me tonight? The weather has promised to remain perfect."

"If you like."

He shrugged. "Ah. We've exhausted two subjects already. That leaves us cabbages and kings. Do you have strong feelings about either?"

"I only know about cabbages," she answered.

"And what do you know?"

"That they're dull." She smiled.

"Then what shall we speak of, if not how lovely you are? Knickknacks? Objets d'art?" He picked up the black enameled vase and examined its intricate gold pattern. "Nice, this. Heavy devil. What is it, exactly?"

Whatever spell has been weaving itself in the afternoon sunshine broke. Kimberly shifted uncomfortably. "Oh," she said uneasily. "That's Grandfather. His ashes, I mean. In the vase."

Alec's face went slightly taut. He set the vase down gingerly. "Your grandfather? G'day, mate! Sorry. Didn't mean to be familiar. Didn't expect the old boy to be hanging about still."

Kimberly shrugged, biting the corner of her mouth. "He was determined that even death wouldn't keep him out of the middle of things. We don't usually mention it—it can put a damper on things."

"You're not having a go at me, are you?" he asked, nodding at the vase and frowning. "That's really him?"

Kimberly nodded. "I'm afraid so. I tried to talk Dodo into putting the container some place less conspicuous, but she said the colonel always insisted he wanted his ashes in *that* vase and on *that* shelf. In fact, he built that shelf for the very purpose."

Alec kept staring at the black vase. He had gone extremely still, like a cat studying its prey. "What did you say?" he demanded, his voice careful.

"He built the whole fireplace. He put that shelf of stone in especially so—so that his ashes could rest there in the vase. I told you he was eccentric. You're starting to see."

It was almost as if he'd forgotten she was in the room. He stared at the large, dark stone that jutted from the face of the fireplace. Its surface was duller and less interesting than that of the other pieces of quartz. In fact, Kimberly had often wondered why her grandfather, so fascinated by stones, had selected this somber and uninteresting one as his final resting place.

"Good Lord," Alec said softly. He stretch his hand out and touched the stone's pebbly surface. He still gazed at it as if hypnotized. "Good Lord," he repeated and turned to her, his eyes suddenly so intent they were frightening. "Kimberly, what do you know about this stone?" he asked.

She shrugged again. "Nothing. Except it's like cabbage. Sort of dull."

He looked at the surrounding stones, the glistening chunks of quartz. "Where did all this come from?" he asked curtly.

"Some cavern," she answered. "He went all over, collecting rocks for this house. There's a fossil from India over the door, and a dinosaur egg is embedded in the cornerstone. "Why?"

He blinked, as if coming back to himself. "Why—this one's about to come loose."

"Loose?" Kimberly asked. "Really?" She frowned. She rose from the love seat and came to stand beside him.

He turned and her view of the stone was blocked. "Yes," he muttered. "Dangerous. An amateur stonemason should never try to build a fireplace, you know. Containing a fire is difficult. An art, in fact."

He put his hands on her bare arms. He ran them up to her shoulders, then laced his fingers into her hair, tipping her face up to him. "Now what shall I do with you?" he asked, his voice almost a purr. "You've started a fire yourself, and I'm the one who must keep it under control. I'm not sure I can."

He took her face between his hands and bent his head, his lips taking hers with slow and certain deliberation. At the taste and touch of his mouth, Kimberly felt her heart bounding away in happiness. He was tall and warm and hard muscled next to her, and he made her forget about such a cold and irrelevant subject as stones.

He drew back, smiling down. "Run upstairs and get ready. I must take you out in public where I'm forced to behave myself."

She smiled up at him. "And I'm forced to behave myself, too."

His face went serious again. "I suppose you know I think I'm in love with you," he said quietly.

Again her heart seemed to leave her, and the sensation was one of both intense pleasure and odd pain. "I love you, too," she answered. His face was solemn, his eyes intent.

"Never forget that, will you?" he asked, his hands still framing her face.

"Never."

He bent and kissed her, softly and quickly. "Go, love," he said. He stepped back, leaning against the fireplace again. Kimberly flashed him a dazzling smile and, turning, left him standing there.

He listened to her light footsteps on the stairs. The trust in her face, he thought darkly. The happiness and trust in her beautiful face. He'd hoped to spare her any hurt. Now there was no way he could not hurt her, and the aunt, too. Up until this moment, he'd had a chance. Now there was no choice.

He turned and looked once more at the dark stone on which the vase rested. "You old fox," he said between his teeth. "Thought you'd keep it for bloody ever, did you?" He reached out and touched the stone again. He'd found it at last. It was disguised, but it was whole, and it was here— the great topaz stolen almost half a century ago, the jewel that had ruined his grandfather, his father, and now threatened to ruin him. The Heart of the Sun.

CHAPTER NINE

HE THOUGHT he'd never seen anything lovelier than when she came downstairs in a whirl of white. She wore a simple halter dress with a wide white belt that set off the smallness of her waist, the fullness of her breasts and hips.

Her only ornaments were the crescent brooch her aunt had given her and the gold earrings that had been Calvin's gift. Her hair fell to her hips, a thick silken cape.

"You're perfect," he said huskily. "Kimberly in the veils of her hair." He put one hand behind her neck, settled it lightly on her nape.

Dodo bustled into the hallway. "Kimberly," she said. "You look lovely, dear. Have a good time."

"And what are you up to, Miss Simpson?" Alec asked with a smile. She had a worn but snow-white tablecloth folded in her arms, and atop it a pair of heavy earthenware plates.

"Oh," Dodo said, not meeting his eyes. "Since it's just Calvin and me tonight, I thought we might have sort of a picnic on the front porch."

As Alec opened the door of the convertible for Kimberly, he said in a low voice, "Picnics on the porch. Don't tell me your aunt is getting romantic."

"My aunt," Kimberly stated firmly, "is trying to be proper. Showing the world that nothing is going on at dinner except dinner—I'm sure."

"What a pity. I think every day he's more taken with her."

"I think you're right."

"That makes two of us poor blokes," he replied, getting in and starting the engine. "Caught in the wiles of the Simpson women."

"I have no wiles," protested Kimberly. "And neither does Dodo."

He gave her an intent blue glance. "That's the most maddening wile of all—an absence of wiles. It could drive a man stark mad."

He smiled at her, but the set of his jaw was rigid. He lapsed into quiet. He was bothered about something, Kimberly realized, deeply bothered. But she couldn't guess what or why.

The Paradise was a French restaurant, set into a little jut of cliff on Spring Street. One entered the front door, climbed a few stairs and walked through the main dining room. Then there was a back door and an outdoor dining room on a stoney plateau of the mountain. Tables with white cloths were set on this large, natural balcony. A cascade of vines and ferns draped the dramatic rise of the mountainside, which formed a back wall of stone.

Alec ordered a bottle of Mumm's champagne, because, he said, it was a special occasion. But even when the cork was popped, he kept his thoughtful, almost dissatisfied expression.

The seriousness with which he kept eyeing her throughout dinner made her almost uncomfortable. Did he regret telling her that he loved her? Perhaps she shouldn't have said that she loved him, too. But she felt incapable of denying it.

"Tell me," he said, looking into the depths of his champagne flute. "Your aunt. You're terribly fond of her..."

"Of course," Kimberly answered. "I mean, I hardly remember my mother. Dodo raised me."

"And family is everything to her, is it not?"

Kimberly nodded. "I think that's part of the reason she started the bed-and-breakfast business—without someone to care for, she felt lost."

"And her father's memory—it means a good deal to her?"

"Almost everything, I guess," she said. "She dedicated most of her life to him. Despite his faults she thought he hung the moon—that he was an extraordinarily special human being."

A muscle flexed in his cheek, giving him a grim look. "And you?" he asked, then took a sip of wine.

Her mouth took on a wry line. "He was extraordinary, all right. An extraordinary old tyrant, I thought."

"But your aunt would be devastated to learn he was a less than exemplary character?"

"Oh, she'd never believe it," Kimberly stated simply. "If she did believe it, it'd probably destroy her. I told you, she lived for him."

He inhaled deeply. His teeth were set as if in determination. "And you would despise anyone who hurt your aunt, of course."

"I'd kill them," she answered frankly. "Dodo's never hurt anyone in her life. Hurting her would be a sin, like tearing the wings off a butterfly."

"Kill them," he mused, glancing up at the darkening mountainside. "Yes. I forgot. You are, after all, the colonel's granddaughter. A woman of temperament."

"A resemblance has been pointed out," Kimberly admitted unhappily. Whenever she had been stubborn or rebellious as a child, Dodo would declare, "I swear, Kimberly, you're just like him.'' It had been a fail-proof method for making her behave.

"But you're also like her," he observed, watching her carefully. "Like your aunt. You're basically an unselfish little creature. And, I hope, a forgiving one." The lines of his face were taut, and something almost fierce shone in his eyes.

"I don't know," she said uneasily. "Why are you asking all this?"

The waiter came, clearing the table. He asked if they wanted any dessert, but Kimberly was suddenly no longer hungry. Alec dismissed him.

He tented his fingers together and stared at her with absorption. "Kimberly," he said, as if he were selecting his words with great care. "I was thinking of going away."

The evening seemed to go suddenly cold. The air felt darker, thicker, hard to breathe. "What?" she asked.

"Away," he repeated, watching her reaction. "Back to Australia. There's illness in the family. It's serious."

"Oh," she said.

"My father," he continued. "He hasn't much longer. I thought I should cancel this trip and go home."

"I—I'm sorry to hear it," she said mechanically. She was swept by loss, shame and confusion. She should be more concerned about his father, but all she could feel was dismay that Alec might leave her.

"This afternoon," he went on relentlessly, "I thought, perhaps, although it's soon for such a thing, I might ask you to wait for me."

"Wait?" she repeated numbly. She looked up at him. Was there hope after all?

He reached into the pocket of his pale blue shirt. He set a small velvet box before her. "This was to be your birthday present," he muttered. "If you'd have it. It was to be a symbol. That I would come back."

He nodded curtly, a signal for her to open the box. Within was a ring set with an enormous deep blue star sapphire. She looked at the ring and then at him, her lips slightly parted.

"A sapphire stands for devotion," he stated, and the muscle in his jaw leaped again. "You must understand that. It's important."

She nodded weakly but was not quite sure she understood anything.

"But when you came down the stairs tonight, I realized that I don't want you to wait for me."

"Oh," she breathed again.

"Kimberly," he said, putting his hand over hers and holding it so tightly that it hurt. "Instead, I want you now. To marry me. Tonight."

"What?" she asked in disbelief. "What?"

"Marry me." His voice was almost brutal. "Now. Tonight. There's a place just over the state border. I'd still have to go back to Australia. And I couldn't take you. Don't ask why. But I'd know you were mine, and I'd be back for you. As soon as I could."

"I—I can't do that," she said helplessly.

"Why not?" he demanded. "I know this has all come about quickly, but I love you. You said you love me."

She made an impotent gesture. "I can't just—run off—it's not right."

"Your aunt?" he asked, squeezing her hand harder still. The set of his mouth was almost fierce.

Kimberly nodded again. She remembered what Dodo had said the night before, about Kimberly leaving the house in daylight, not slipping away by night as her mother had in that ill-advised and ill-fated marriage.

"Listen," he said. "Your aunt wants you to live your own life. You know it's true."

She stared at him, bewildered. "But just to run off—how would I ever tell her?"

"Don't tell her at all," he offered, shrugging contemptuously. "Don't tell her until I come back for you. I don't want to wait for you. I want you. Now. All of you."

The turbulence and passion in his voice made her shiver slightly. "It wouldn't be right," she protested shakily.

"Damn the idea of *right*," he swore, staring into her eyes. "This is more important than any *right*. It's important that you understand that, too."

Tears sprang to her eyes. "I *don't* understand," she insisted. "I don't understand anything. When are you going? Why can't you take me?"

"Soon," he replied. "In a few days at the most. I can't take you, that's all. I told you, don't ask. Come with me tonight instead. I want to hold you all night long—with you wearing only the veils of your beautiful hair."

"And where would we do this?" she asked, just as passionately. "In my room or yours? With the Fremont sisters right next door and Dodo listening from her room and knowing—"

"What difference does it make, where?" he retorted. "We'll find a hotel, a motel, what does it matter?"

"It does matter," she answered. "Can't *you* understand? It sounds so squalid, somehow—we slip over the border to some marriage mill and then spend our wedding night in the first hotel we come across—and then come home and *lie* about it?"

He picked up his napkin and threw it on the table. The muscle in his cheek was jerking like a fast pulse now. "Tell her the truth, then. What does it matter? What difference do the blithering details make, anyway? Unless, of course, you don't love me. Don't tell me you still have that silly jackass in Kansas City on your mind."

Kimberly almost laughed. Roger seemed less substantial than a phantom to her. What she'd felt for him had been merely infatuation, and a mild infatuation at that, compared with the intensity of her feeling for Alec.

"I do love you," she answered, suddenly more confused than before. If she loved him, then wasn't there truth in what he said? It wouldn't matter where they were married, only that they were. It wouldn't matter where they made love for the first time, only that they belonged to each other, completely and forever.

Seeing the conflict and dismay on her face, he held up his hand, as if in a signal to halt. "All right," he said, an impatient slant to his mouth. "All right. Don't give me an answer now. Think it over tonight. Tomorrow, marry me—or don't. Decide—" he picked up the box with the ring "—if this is to be your wedding ring or only something you'll remember me by, while a great sea is between us."

He snapped the box shut. "Take it," he ordered. "And decide."

She shook her head. "No. You keep it." She almost whispered it. She was afraid if she touched the ring, she would be lost; she would simply put her hand in his and go wherever he wished, do whatever he wanted. Already she regretted refusing, even for one night.

"Tell your aunt beforehand, too, if you want," he said between his teeth. "She'll advise you to wait. But waiting, Kimberly, is for the timid. I don't think it's for you, and I know it's not for me."

Kimberly turned her face away, staring at the vines and ferns that cloaked the rocks. "My mother ran off and got married," she said softly. "At some shabby little justice of the peace. She was afraid to go home or tell the colonel. He reported her missing. It wasn't a very nice way to start a marriage. I'd want it—different.''

"They were two other people," he replied. He shook his head in displeasure. "They weren't us." He gave a short bitter laugh. "Well. Ruined your birthday, haven't I? But what's a twenty-first birthday for, if not for great decisions to be made? Or perhaps it's no great decision for you at all."

She cast him a dark glance. Coolly, his eyes held hers. "I don't want you to go away," she said at last. "I don't want you to leave."

"My love," he said calmly, raising his wineglass, "I have no choice."

He signalled for the check. "And what," he asked cynically, "shall I do with you now, indecisive maiden that you are? I can't take you dancing. If I hold you in my arms, I'll not dance, I promise you that. A show, perhaps? People who live in tourist towns never seem to have seen the tourist attractions, right? A real New Yorker wouldn't be caught going through the Statue of Liberty, all that sort of thing."

He stood and stretched his hand out to her. He looked down at her with a mixture of desire and exasperation. "Come on, Kimberly," he said. "Let's waste time, the better to pretend that we have all we'll ever need."

She took his hand and rose, looking into his eyes. None of this seemed quite real. He took her to a musical show where she really didn't see or hear what happened on the stage. Events happened before her, but they did not register in her brain. She sat stunned throughout it all.

Alec did not so much as hold her hand. Occasionally he allowed his arm to rest on the back of her seat, and once his fingers toyed with a silken strand of her hair. But he stopped himself, almost immediately.

Afterward, they had another drink at a small sidewalk café. Alec purposely kept his talk inconsequential. It was as if the earlier conversation about marriage had never taken place.

He kept up the same desultory conversation as he drove her home and walked her to the door. He stopped on the porch. "I'm not coming in for a while, Kimberly," he said, looking down at her. "I think it's best I not. Think about what I asked you. You can tell me your decision tomorrow."

He isn't even going to touch me, Kimberly thought in disappointment. She stood in silence, looking up at his shadowy features, the faint light of the street lamp glimmering on his hair.

Then he swept her into his arms and gave her one long, eloquent kiss. His hands moved over her bare shoulders, tangled themselves in the thick wealth of her hair. His lips seemed to mate with hers, driving all else from her mind.

He crushed her close to him, and his mouth ravished hers. Every sort of aching sensual pleasure seemed to swim through her blood, and half-faint, she clung to the taut strength of him. Then his mouth was on her throat, the curve of her jaw, the corner of her winglike brow.

His hands moved over the bare flesh of her back and arms with a maddening combination of ferocity and tenderness. Kimberly gasped and stood shakily on tiptoe, so that he might embrace her even more intimately. There was a tightly controlled savagery in him, a hunger held barely in check.

Kimberly shuddered, need vibrating through her body. "You see," he said against her ear, his lips nibbling and kissing her silky skin between the words, "you see why it's best I don't come in."

With a ragged breath he stepped back, holding her almost at arm's length from him. His hands gripped her by the elbows. In the summery darkness, he looked at her for a long moment. His hands dropped away at last.

"Tomorrow," he said. Then he turned on his booted heel and was down the stairs. He vaulted into the car, not bothering to open the door. He bent over the ignition, starting the motor.

Kimberly stood, her lips stinging sweetly. Every nerve in her body seemed to vibrate. Wait, she wanted to cry. Don't go! Take me with you, now. Now. *I'll go with you.* Anywhere.

But the force of her emotions had shaken her too much. She opened her lips, but nothing came out. She heard the car growl to life. Then Alec was gone.

She half sighed, half sobbed. She threw her head back and looked out at the stars. They seemed to dance and spin, making her dizzy. Trembling, she stepped inside. In the living room another shudder of desire and confusion surged over her. She leaned her forehead against the cool stone of the fireplace, letting her fingers trace its comforting solidity.

Her breathing slowed to normal at last.

SOMETIME during the night, a sound rang out from downstairs. It was a sort of sharp metallic clang that woke Kimberly immediately. It was followed by a second, almost identical sound. Sleepily, she sat up in bed.

She heard the opening of a door, the soft scurry of footsteps. "What is it?" she heard Dodo call timorously. "Who's there? If you're a burglar, we have nothing. Go away—one of the guests here is a visiting policeman! A great big one!"

A familiar voice came up the stairs, rising out of the darkness. "It's Alec, Miss Simpson. Don't be alarmed. I didn't want to turn on the lights, and I banged into something. Sorry."

"Oh, my goodness," said Dodo, her voice relieved. "I thought it was the crack of doom. It's all right, Mr. Shaughnessy. You just gave me a start."

Kimberly yawned pleasurably. She pulled the crisp sheet up around her neck. How unlike Alec to do something clumsy, she thought sleepily. He was as graceful as a cat. Perhaps his emotions were as turbulent as her own had been tonight.

She yawned again. Alec, she thought dreamily. She would go to him tomorrow. She had known it as soon as he had kissed her good-night. This time tomorrow night she would be married.

Married, she thought with languid bliss, burrowing more deeply into the softness of the bed. Alec, she thought happily, and drifted off to dreams of him, the strange noise in the night forgotten.

"YES, QUITE A CRACK IN THE MORTAR," Alec said, showing Dodo and Kimberly the long, snaking flaw in the fireplace. He looked lean and fit in his faded jeans and white shirt, but his face still looked haggard. "Definitely needs replacing."

"How odd I didn't notice before." Dodo frowned, looking concerned. "I dust every day."

Alec shrugged. "It's only a hairline crack, but a deep one. It may have just appeared. They do, as a house settles, you know."

"Dear, dear," Dodo murmured, shaking her head. "Now we'll have to send for the stone mason, I suppose."

"No need," Alec said smoothly. "I can chip the mortar out, replace the stone. The pressure's made the stone crack, too."

"Oh, dear," Dodo exclaimed, "Where?"

"There," Alec said, pointing at a seam in the stone's rugged surface. "The thing might just sheer off someday and dump this lovely vase on the floor."

"That would never do," Dodo stated, shaking her head. "That's—well, it's not an ordinary vase."

Alec turned and gave Kimberly a slow, private smile. She smiled back, noting Dodo's delicate reluctance to admit the truth about the vase. "Here, then," he said gently. "You'd better put it someplace safe until I have this thing fixed."

He handed the vase to Dodo, who took it, carefully, bearing it to the hall closet and putting it on the top shelf.

How peculiar, Kimberly thought, that they all stood in the living room, talking about something as dull as the fireplace, when their lives were on the brink of such tremendous change.

"I can fix it in a trice," Alec said casually. "I'll just need another stone. And after breakfast, I'll take a polaroid picture, so I get everything just right, how far it juts out and so forth."

"I thought you said an amateur shouldn't try to fix a fireplace," Kimberly offered. She hated seeing him do all these dreary tasks, no matter how badly they needed doing.

He cocked an eyebrow. "I said one shouldn't try to build one. But a little job like this? I can patch it up quickly enough."

"You are just the nicest man," Dodo said, with a gentle cluck of her tongue. "It's like a gift from heaven. I'm going to make you a special breakfast."

"It's nothing," Alec replied. For a fleeting moment Kimberly thought he looked uncomfortable. But it must have been a trick of the morning light. Immediately he seemed his usual smiling and slightly cynical self.

Dodo made a succulent breakfast, so delicious even the Fremont sisters, who were to depart today, raved about it.

That, Kimberly thought wryly, was quite an accomplishment.

After breakfast, the sisters went upstairs to pack. Calvin hadn't yet arrived, and Alec insisted Dodo and Kimberly leave their task of clearing the table for a moment. He took several pictures of them by the fireplace. Kimberly couldn't keep from smiling. She wondered if whoever married them would be kind enough to take a photo of them at their wedding.

Alec left, to get some equipment, he said, and to go to the rock shop to find a substitute for the cracked stone. The Fremont sisters left, declaring that they'd had a most memorable time and might return next summer, if Dodo promised the quality of the cooking would remain the same.

Dodo sighed with weary satisfaction when they left. No new guests were due for another two days—there would be a brief respite from hard labor. She and Kimberly did the dishes. Then, just as the last cup was hung up and the last saucer stacked, Dodo's hands flew to her cheeks, and her eyes filled with bewilderment.

"Oh, Kimberly," she said, her voice filled with guilt. "I have something to tell you. I carried it around all day yesterday, meaning to give it to you in private. But then you were gone, and it completely slipped my mind."

She went to the big wooden bread box, opened it and withdrew a long envelope that was yellowed with age. "How could I forget?" Dodo asked herself, shaking her head. "I made a sacred promise—oh, I'm such a flibbertigibbet."

Kimberly shook her head so that her long hair swung. "Don't carry on so," she said. "Yesterday wasn't exactly an ordinary day—" she paused, wondering if now was the time to tell her aunt about Alec's proposal.

Dodo turned, her eyes sad and serious. "This isn't just an ordinary letter, either," she said. "This was to be given to you on your twenty-first birthday. It's from your mother, dear."

She handed Kimberly the envelope, which was thick, as if it contained several pages. "My mother?" Kimberly's voice was quiet with disbelief.

"She wrote it before she died," Dodo said, clasping her hands in concern. "And I promised to give it to you the day you turned twenty-one—"

"It's all right, Dodo." Kimberly consoled her by adding, "It's only a day late—just a matter of hours, really."

The letter gave her a slightly ominous feeling for reasons she did not understand. It was a bit too much like a communication from the grave. She thought again of the rhyme of prophecy Alec had told her. "A gift, a ghost, a friend, a foe, a letter to come, a journey to go."

There'd already been the gift of the ring, and Alec's journey home, and now the letter. She supposed she should take it to the privacy of her room to read.

But there was a loud, familiar knock at the front door. Calvin had arrived. Kimberly went to let him in. "Good morning, Calvin," she said and started upstairs.

"I have to talk to you," he asserted. "You and Dodo both. It's important."

Calvin's ruddy face was unnaturally grim. A disturbed look dwelt deep in his gray eyes. He had removed his hat and stood holding it before him, as if this were some solemn occasion, such as a funeral.

He cast a concerned glance first at Kimberly, then at Dodo, who appeared at the door of the dining room. "I think we'd better sit down," he said at last. "Maybe have some coffee if you've got any ready," he nodded to Dodo. "We may need something to brace us."

"My goodness," Dodo said, her hand rising to her lips. "What is it?"

Kimberly wondered, herself. Calvin looked so worried, so uncomfortable that she was concerned. Perhaps, she thought, he was going to propose to Dodo. No, she thought, no amount of shyness on earth could make a man look that unhappy. She slipped the envelope into the pocket of her green sundress.

Dodo set out cups and filled them with the last of the breakfast coffee. She and Kimberly sat down at the table. "Now," said Dodo, "whatever is the matter, Calvin?"

He took a drink of black coffee. He wiped his mustache with a napkin. He looked at Dodo, then he looked at Kimberly.

"It's your Mr. Shaughnessy," he said, his eyes not wavering from Kimberly's. "He's lying to you. He's lied to us all from the beginning."

CHAPTER TEN

"Lied?" Dodo cried incredulously. "Lied? About what?"

"About everything," Calvin replied, his eyes still fastened on Kimberly's. "The man probably hasn't told the truth about one thing since he's been here."

Calvin's words seared into her brain. She sat numbly, her coffee in front of her, forgotten. Surely Calvin was mistaken. For if Alec had lied about everything, then he had lied about loving her.

"He's always bothered me," Calvin went on relentlessly. He cast a concerned glance at Dodo, then stared meditatively into the depths of his coffee cup. "He was too interested in the old stories about this house—and the death of the rajah."

"But," Kimberly struggled to protest, "he's a folklorist. It's his business to be interested in old stories—"

"He's not," Calvin returned abruptly. "At least he's not who or what he says. I called Australia last night. What has he told you? He's a professor in Brisbane?"

Kimberly nodded.

"There's no listing in Brisbane for any Professor Alec Shaughnessy," Calvin said gruffly.

"That doesn't mean anything," Kimberly protested desperately. "He was going to be here all summer. He probably had his phone shut off—"

"I called the university, Kimberly," Calvin told her. "They'd never heard of any Alec Shaughnessy. And neither had any other college or university anywhere near."

"He—he—there's some mistake," Kimberly argued. She felt odd and sick, as if her life were leaving her body through some unseen wound.

"I did talk to a folklorist in Brisbane," Calvin muttered, forging ahead. "He asked me why anybody'd come around here to collect folklore, anyway. He said there was book after book on this area by a man named Vance Randolph. And that Randolph was probably the greatest folklorist this country ever produced."

Kimberly's mind veered drunkenly. She remembered the name, Vance Randolph—she had even seen his books in the book store. "But those books have been around forever," she countered, trying to think straight. "Alec could have come for new material—"

"I said the same thing," Calvin retorted between clenched teeth. "But he said the lore is dying out here—good heaven, Kimberly, I'm proof of that. Who's around to sing the old songs of the hills? Me—an old phony from Pasadena, who just happens to like the music. There *is* no new material. None worth speaking of."

Kimberly sat, unable to say anything. She shook her head, as if the gesture would deny Calvin's words.

Dodo was looking at her in concern. "This is terrible," Dodo breathed. "If he isn't who he says he is, who is he? What does he want?"

"I don't know," Calvin answered, watching Dodo's reaction. "But I have some guesses. He wants something you've got. Or that he thinks you've got."

"What?" Dodo asked in dismay. "We have nothing—this house—the furniture—a few odd pieces from India, but that's all. Why, until Kimberly came home, I didn't know how I was going to keep this house going—''

"Listen, both of you," Calvin said, then took a deep breath. He looked like a man who has steeled himself to perform some extremely unpleasant task. "Yesterday afternoon when he was gone, I looked in the attic. There was no sign of any squirrels or animals being up there. Ever. Believe me, I'd know. Instead, I think he's been going over every trunk, box and file stored up there—very carefully and very thoroughly."

"What?" cried Dodo, appalled.

"I'm sure that's what you heard from there in the night," Calvin gritted out. "Him. And he made sure he got up there in the day time, too, just to make sure he searched it completely."

"But what for?" Dodo asked. "It's mostly old papers— the colonel's records—the household budgets, his investments—''

"He was looking for something," Calvin said, shaking his head in disgust. "And he kept looking. He was doing more than helping repair things in this house. He was combing it, floor by floor, inch by inch."

Kimberly put her elbow on the table and clamped her hand over her mouth. Tears stung her eyes. She shook her head again, not wanting to hear Calvin or believe him.

"You knew yesterday afternoon?" Dodo asked. She, too, looked numb. "You should have told us then, Calvin. Oh, why didn't you?"

He looked unhappy and hangdog. "It was Kimberly's birthday. And I didn't know then that he was going under a false identity—or at least a false story. When I found out, everything started falling together." He gave Kimberly a searching look. "I'm sorry, Kimberly," he growled. "I could see you becoming more and more caught up by him."

Dodo rose from her chair and went to Kimberly. She stood behind her and put her hands on her shoulders. "I'm here," she said to Kimberly simply. "I will always be here when you need me. We'll get through this together."

Kimberly barely kept her self-possession. She put her right hand over Dodo's. Her jaw quivered and tears glimmered in her eyes, but she refused to cry.

Dodo squeezed her niece's shoulders comfortingly. She smoothed her hair. She looked across the table, meeting Calvin's troubled gaze. "What is he looking for?" she demanded calmly. "What does he want?"

Calvin shrugged helplessly. He seemed to search for words. "Frankly," he said at last, "I think it's about that jewel. The topaz. The Heart of the Sun. He thinks it's here."

Dodo's hands went still on Kimberly's shoulders. "That's ridiculous," she insisted. "Sir Cyril Damon stole it years ago and took it to Canada. It's never been seen again. It's probably been cut into a hundred pieces."

Calvin flexed his big hands. He stared down at them. "Dodo," he said firmly, "the man seems certain it's here. Why else his interest in it? Why the deception? Why the search?"

"But it couldn't be here," Dodo returned earnestly. "That would mean that the colonel had it instead of Sir Cyril. And that's impossible because it would mean that—"

She stopped speaking, clearly unable to utter the thought. Calvin regarded her solemnly. He finished it for her. "That would mean the colonel killed the rajah and took the gem."

"No!" Dodo said in horror. "No!" She moved weakly away from Kimberly. She sank into her chair again. To Kimberly's distress, Dodo put her head between her hands and began to weep softly.

Calvin looked terrible, like a man who has destroyed something irreplaceable. "It only means that Shaughnessy thinks so," he said, his tone almost pleading. "After all, the stories have circulated for years. You're not going to let them get to you now, are you?"

Wordlessly, Dodo shook her head but kept her face covered and kept on weeping. "Dodo." Calvin consoled her helplessly. "Now, Dodo. I'm sorry. I'm sorry—dear." He took one of her hands in his big one and patted it awkwardly.

"That he could lie so—not to me—but to Kimberly," Dodo managed to sob at last. She dug into her pocket for her handkerchief.

Dodo broke into fresh tears and Calvin stood and made her stand, too. "There, there," he said and put his arms around her. "Now, now."

Kimberly looked at them. She had never seen Dodo so distraught, not even when the colonel died. To see her aunt so unhappy was like having her heart ripped in two. Kimberly was grateful for Calvin's bearish tenderness, his deep concern. He loved Dodo, that was clear. That's what love was, something quiet and steady and deep. It wasn't like what she felt for Alec. That was a kind of madness. He had said as much himself. Madness. It had led her here, to this terrible moment.

She wanted to be alone. Dodo, whether she knew it yet or not, was in the best of hands. Calvin might not be handsome or rich, but he was good, and he was kind.

"I'm going upstairs," she said. She seemed to be viewing events from a great distance, and she was benumbed, so nothing really hurt too badly. It was a little like being dead, she supposed.

Then she heard Alec's car pull up. Calvin heard it, too. "It's him," he said grimly. He patted Dodo's back. "What do you want me to do? I'll beat the devil out of him, if you want."

A gallant offer, Kimberly thought coldly, but a foolish one. Calvin was four inches shorter than Alec, thirty years older, and he carried most of his weight in his midsection. "No," she said, rising. She would meet Alec herself.

Dodo straightened in Calvin's arms. "No, Kimberly," she said with surprising conviction. "You'll have your say. But first I'll speak to him."

Calvin looked at her doubtfully, but Dodo lifted her chin, wiped her eyes and blew her nose. She squeezed her handkerchief tightly, squared her shoulders and marched to the front door.

Calvin followed her closely, his fists clenched, just in case. Kimberly felt as though she were drifting behind them, detached somehow from the whole scene.

Alec, a few packages in the crook of his bronzed arm, swung open the front door. Dodo, her back like a ramrod, barred his way. "I don't want you in my house, Mr. Shaughnessy," she said, her voice like that of a small but very powerful queen. "You are no longer welcome. Especially after the way you've acted toward my niece. What you've tried to do to me is of little consequence. But the way you've acted toward her is unforgivable. Unforgivable."

Alec stopped in the open doorway. He looked down at Dodo. He looked at Calvin, and his blue eyes suddenly flashed fire. The two men stared at each other for an interminable moment. Then Alec's gaze moved to Kimberly. The muscle that always twitched in his cheek when he was holding himself in check jerked dangerously. "Kimberly?" he said. "What's happened?"

"Get out," Kimberly said between her teeth. "I never want to see you again. Liar!"

"Kimberly," he repeated, warning in his voice.

"I said, get out—I never want to see you again." Her own frigid calm amazed her. She was in shock of some kind, she supposed.

"Oh, you'll want to see me again," he said insolently. "It's not over this easily. Don't lie to yourself."

She turned so she wouldn't have to look at him any longer. Something, she thought, was starting to break inside her. She could feel it. And it was going to hurt a great deal.

"Two ladies have told you to leave," Calvin threatened. "Get out before I throw you out."

There was a long moment of silence. The air in the room almost crackled. Alec finally smiled. Decades of bitterness seemed to shine in that smile. "No," he stated. He looked down at Dodo. Gently he put his hands on her shoulders. "Not until I get what I've come for."

"Don't touch her," Calvin warned, and Kimberly whirled, outraged to see Alec's hands still on her aunt's slender shoulders.

"Miss Simpson," Alec said, bending so that Dodo could look him straight in the eye. "I lied because I had no choice. I lied to find truth, and the truth is this—the Heart of the Sun is here. In this house. It has been for years."

Calvin had begun to move toward Alec. "Calvin—don't!" Dodo ordered in fright. The older man stopped, staring in perplexity. Dodo looked back at Alec, raising her chin. "The Heart of the Sun is gone," she said in challenge. "It was stolen by Sir Cyril Damon."

"Sir Cyril didn't steal it, Miss Simpson," Alec contradicted, his eyes piercing. "Although he paid for it—all his life—and so did his children. But he never had it. It's here. It always has been."

"Don't badger her," Calvin ordered, his face reddening. "Or you'll answer to me."

"But she," Alec said, his cold smile flashing at Calvin, "must answer to her conscience, mustn't she?"

Dodo's back grew even straighter. "The stone is not here, Mr. Shaughnessy—or whoever you are. It has never been here."

"But it has, madame," he corrected her. "And I tell you, I know where. It's in the fireplace."

Kimberly stared at him. The ice seemed to have spread from her brain now and encased her whole body. Yet she had a peculiar sense of the truth breaking through. It made so many things suddenly clear—her grandfather's settling in this obscure little town, his increasing reclusiveness, the odd house, the fireplace with its special stone shelf.

Alec was right. The jewel was there. And he had come to steal it.

"The fireplace," she said, with no emotion at all in her voice. "Of course."

"It can't be," Dodo returned, suddenly sounding frightened.

"I can show you," Alec told her, still gripping her shoulders. "A man has the right to defend himself when people speak against him. I say any crime of mine is small compared to the crime that was done long ago."

"He's right," Kimberly said coldly, not caring any longer what happened. Pieces fell into place for her. He had been going to steal the stone. How could he protect himself more cleverly than by marrying her? She couldn't testify against him if he were her husband—wasn't that the law? She didn't understand its intricacies. Perhaps by marrying her he'd even have some claim to the stone. Or perhaps he'd simply wanted to humiliate her. It didn't matter now. He had made fools of both her and Dodo, but especially of her.

"Let him come in, Dodo," Kimberly said, her voice harsh with resentment. "Let him prove himself. It still doesn't excuse him. He's a liar and was going to be a thief."

"He won't prove it because he can't," Dodo said, but her voice shook. "Step inside, Mr. Shaughnessy. Show us where this treasure is supposedly hidden. It will be another of your lies. One that you have unfortunately come to believe."

"Dodo," Calvin said, his voice strained, "are you sure you want—"

"Let him do his worst," Dodo almost cried. She stepped aside. "My father was not a thief."

Kimberly watched as Alec strode into the front room. He gave the three of them a cool look. "We'll see," he said.

"Is your name even really Shaughnessy?" Calvin growled.

"Yes." Alec took a power chisel from one of the parcels he had carried. He began unwrapping the cord.

"What are you?" Calvin demanded. "I know you're not a folklorist."

"I'm not a professional jewel thief, either," Alec bit off. "Or I'd have made a better job of it, wouldn't I? I'm a director—documentary films mostly. I wasn't even certain what to look for once I knew the stone was here. I kept checking descriptions with the university library, making appointments with geologists, hoping to find out. And yesterday—thanks to Kimberly—I found it. Unprepossessing as it looks on the surface."

He plugged the tool in and thrust the chisel deep into the crack that snaked below the dark stone. He turned it on. It made a terrible grinding roar.

Mortar showered down. Alec moved the chisel, grinding away the mortar that held neighboring stones in place. The dreadful noise growled on. Kimberly still seemed to be viewing things from a long way off. It hardly mattered to her that Alec was destroying the fireplace, the showpiece of the room. She understood now the noise he had made last night. Somehow he had contrived to strike the fireplace so that the crack appeared. More deception.

The chisel yammered maniacally. Another cascade of mortar rained down. He shut the tool off at last and lay it down. "There," he said with grim satisfaction. He took a regular chisel and pried away the stone above the dark one. "You can see."

Both Dodo and Kimberly stood still. It was Calvin who suddenly seemed in charge. He stepped to the fireplace and peered at the part of the stone freshly exposed. "My God," he said.

"The Heart of the Sun," Alec told him. "Doctored. Disguised. Hidden for over four decades. Hidden here."

Calvin's weathered face looked abnormally pale. "I've never seen anything like it," he breathed. "That's not quartz—it's some kind of jewel."

"Yes," Alec said bitterly. "A very large topaz."

"How did you know?" Kimberly asked. The timbre of her own voice surprised her. It sounded calm, icy.

"My name is Alec Shaughnessy," he returned, his tone as cool as hers. "But my father's was Alec Damon—before he changed it. Sir Cyril was my grandfather. He was ruined by what happened in India. He took his sons from England and relocated in Canada. Then he tried Australia. He died there, unwept, unhonored and unsung. Except by his sons."

"Your grandfather," Kimberly said in defiance and contempt, "was a murderer."

"No." His words flicked out like the strokes of a whip. "Yours was. And a thief to boot. The proof is here."

"No," Dodo said in a weak voice. "Please!" Her knees buckled. Her body started to sag.

"Dodo!" cried Calvin. He stepped forward, catching her in his arms. He picked her up.

"I'm all right," she said weakly, but clearly she was not. He carried her to the love seat. He stretched her out. "I'm all right," she repeated, but she was frighteningly pale. Calvin knelt at her side.

For the first time concern crossed Alec's face. He stepped toward the love seat.

"No!" Kimberly said, stepping between Alec and her aunt. "Stay away. What do you want—to make sure you destroy her?"

He reached out, trying to take Kimberly by the arms. She slapped savagely at his hands. "Kimberly, I had to," he said, his face taut. "My father's dying. He's lived a life in exile and disgrace. He wants to go home—to England one last time. He wants to die there. But only if the family name is cleared."

"Then go home and clear it," she told him between clenched teeth. She drew back her hand and slapped him with all her force across the face.

He did not flinch. He simply stared down at her. "I hope your aunt will be fine," he murmured. "I never wanted to hurt her. Or you. I hoped the bloody jewel wasn't here. But it was. I did what I had to."

"Get out!" Kimberly stormed. She would have slapped him again, but he caught her by the wrist.

He held her fast, and she was powerless. He stared down at the tumultuous emotions playing in her face and smiled slightly. "Goodbye for now, love," he said. "But I'll be back. About the jewel." He released her. Then he turned abruptly and left.

She turned, too, her whole body shaking, and went to the love seat. She sank down on her knees beside Calvin and stroked her aunt's clammy forehead in concern. "Is she all right? Will she be all right?"

Dodo moaned. She closed her eyes, pain in her face. "Kimberly?"

"I'm here," Kimberly said. "He's gone now. Everything's going to be all right."

"Let's take her into the bedroom," Calvin said. "Get some brandy for her. And call a doctor, just in case."

Calvin carried Dodo up the stairs. Kimberly called the doctor, then poured out the brandy. The glass shook in her hand as she carried it upstairs.

TWO HOURS LATER, the doctor had come and gone. Dodo seemed fine, he said, although he would like her to come to his office the next day for a complete checkup. She was alert, if somewhat stunned, but not ready to talk about what happened. He'd given her a tranquilizer, and now she slept upstairs peacefully.

Calvin and Kimberly sat listlessly on the love seat, staring at the fireplace. The dust and rubble of the mortar still lay on the hearth. Neither could quite bear to touch it yet. Both of them had looked at the stone Alec had partially uncovered. The surface had been covered with an aggregate of dark quartz crystals. But where the stone itself could be seen, it gleamed with a fire so deeply gold that it verged on magic.

And yet, Kimberly thought, it could never be worth the sorrow it had cost. She didn't want to think of the Damon family and the years of unjust suffering they had endured. She wanted only to thaw the ice of her shock with the growing, intense fire of her hatred for Alec.

She did hate him, she told herself. He might have killed Dodo. He had lied to them all—he had almost seduced her, almost tricked her into marriage.

"Calvin," she asked unhappily, "who does that—that thing belong to, anyway?" She nodded toward the ravaged fireplace. "The house is Dodo's and mine. Does that mean, after all these years, the topaz belongs to us? Would it have been part of Alec's if he'd married me?"

"Who knows?" groaned Calvin. "You're talking about things like community property and the statute of limitations—legal mumbo-jumbo. Don't ask me. And don't tell me you were thinking of marrying him, because I've had enough disaster for one day."

Kimberly was silent for a moment. "Calvin," she said, her voice suddenly small. "Do you really think Dodo's all right? That she's going to be all right?"

"Almost one hundred per cent sure, sweet thing," he answered, his bearish tone not hiding the emotion he felt. "She's the original iron butterfly. I always said she was stronger than anybody gave her credit for. Look at you—you're from the same stock as she is."

"I don't feel strong," Kimberly admitted unhappily. "I feel all used up."

He patted her knee awkwardly. "Well, kid, you looked strong. That counts for something. You stood up to Shaughnessy like a one-woman army. The way you hit him—you have a very good right arm."

She opened her right hand and stared down at it. She had actually bruised her fingers when she slapped Alec. "My drawing hand," she said with derision. "I nearly ruined that on him, too." She lapsed into silence, sinking into the depths of her unhappiness and anger.

She might have married him. Maybe that was the final blow he'd meant to deal her on behalf of the Damons—to humiliate her completely, marry and desert her. How could she begin to understand what went on in his mind? She would never let another man so much as touch her. Not as long as she lived. She had learned her lesson at last.

"Kimberly," Calvin said finally. "I suppose it's clear how I feel about Dodo. I've—uh—been attracted to her for years. But I didn't have a thing to offer her. I knew the colonel would shoot me if I ever came near her. I couldn't even have blamed him . . ."

Kimberly looked at him expectantly.

He stared at the ravaged fireplace. "The funny thing is, I used to think maybe she returned my interest—just a little. Sometimes she'd stop and listen to me sing. We'd look at each other, and then we'd look away. That's all. I thought that's all it'd ever be. But things have changed."

He took a deep breath. "About the time the colonel died, my mother died in Pasadena. I came into some money. Hell, I didn't even know what to do with it. Stuck it in the bank—forty thousand dollars. I was used to living the way I lived. I watched how hard Dodo worked, and I thought, 'Well, now, there's nothing to stop me.' But I was afraid to do anything. Until you came back home. I thought it might be all right to come calling, then. But things have happened so fast, and I think, when Dodo recovers from all this, that I'll, well, what I'm trying to say is—"

She reached over and took his big hand in her own. "I know what you're trying to say, Calvin," she said softly. "I think it's wonderful. Ask her. I hope she'll say yes. It would be perfect."

He looked embarrassed, but pleased. "You really think so? You don't think I'm an old fool?"

"I don't even think you're old," she answered, trying to smile. "You and she have a lot of years left. I think it would be marvelous for you to spend them together. She's a very special lady, and you appreciate her."

"If she says yes, I'll take good care of her," Calvin vowed earnestly. "And, Kimberly, I want you to know that there's enough money to take care of you, too. Enough for art school."

"Oh, Calvin," she said, fighting back tears. "I couldn't let you. But it's wonderful of you to offer."

Looking even more deeply embarrassed, Calvin put his arm around her. "I'm getting downright soppy in my old age," he grumbled. "It's scary what love does to you. I'd run for the hills, but it's too late."

Kimberly felt sorrow tearing through her at his words. *It's scary what love does to you.* It was worse than scary, for her. It was terrifying and shameful. She wondered if she would ever feel happy or whole again. No. She could not.

Suddenly, without wanting to, she was weeping like a child against Calvin's shoulder.

"Kimberly," he said, patting her back awkwardly, "Don't. He isn't worth it. He just isn't worth it."

CHAPTER ELEVEN

THE TELEPHONE rang shrilly. Kimberly wiped her eyes on the handkerchief Calvin gave her. Trying to control her voice, she answered the call. Her body went rigid when she recognized Alec's voice.

"How's your aunt?" he demanded. "Is she all right?"

"Yes," Kimberly retorted, her voice shaking. "No thanks to you. Are you disappointed?"

"Don't be a fool," he snapped. "Listen to me. I'm coming for the jewel. I won't be alone. I'll have a barrister with me, and I've contacted the state police. They're sending agents to supervise the removal of the stone. And I'll have a regular stone mason, as well. To ensure the thing gets out in one piece."

"What about reporters?" Kimberly asked acrimoniously. "And a television crew? And a brass band—and a three-ring circus? Why don't you invite the whole state? The whole country? And your whole country, too, while you're at it?"

"Are you finished?" he asked, his voice sardonic.

"I'm surprised you have the courage to come back," she told him. "Aren't you afraid that once they get the stone out, I'll hit you over the head with it and kill you? We're murderer's spawn over here, you know. Desperate women—dangerous pair, Dodo and I. No wonder you tried to keep your tracks covered."

"You're dangerous, all right," he retorted. "More dangerous than you know. I'd like to get you alone—just for five minutes—"

"What do you intend to do with this jewel, anyway?" she asked. "Finance a documentary—Mr. Director? A feature film with us as the villains?"

He swore. "It'll be turned over to authorities. It belongs to the Indian government. Pratap inherited the throne, but when India gained its independence, he was remiss about paying taxes. So it belongs to the people. Perhaps the thing will do some good at last."

She gave a short laugh of disbelief. "What do you care about 'good'?" she asked contemptuously.

"Sometimes one gets into a position where somebody has to be hurt, innocent or not," he returned acidly. "My father is dying. He wanted justice at last. And he wanted to go home to England. Well, now he can go. He'll have his wish. But I had to find what really happened to the stone. What was I to do, walk into your house and say, 'Good day, I'd like to search your house and prove that your venerable ancestor was a lying blackguard?' How was I to know that you and your aunt were any better than he? How was I to do anything except try to give my father his dying wish?"

"Oh, yes," Kimberly said sarcastically. "You're extremely noble."

"Look at it from my side, will you?" he demanded.

She hung up the phone with a crash she hoped would make his ear ring for a week.

He showed up, true to his word, with an entourage.

Calvin glared at Alec as he let the men in. Kimberly glared at them all. The stone mason looked uncomfortable with all the fuss. The lawyer looked self-important and delighted by the entire, confused scene. The state patrolmen, in their uniforms, looked official and professionally impassive.

There was, to Kimberly's humiliation, even a pair of local policemen and the police photographer. Outside was an armored truck to transport the jewel to a secure place.

Neighbors and curious passersby stood outside in clusters, whispering. Kimberly, too restless to watch the removal of the jewel, went upstairs. She unlocked Alec's bedroom door and gathered up his things, stuffing them without ceremony into his suitcases. She took out the box that had found its way back to his bottom drawer. The elephant-faced Ganesha gleamed on its lid.

She stared at the locked box a moment, thinking of how many of her family's secrets he must have pried into as he searched the attic. She hesitated only a moment. She brought down the box against the corner of the desk as hard as she could. The enameled wood split. The small hinges fell away. She opened it.

Within were copies, dozens of photocopies of records written in her grandfather's cramped hand. Alec must have taken the documents from the attic, photocopied them and put the originals back. She looked at them, only half-comprehending their significance. Many of them had to do with investments in mines.

She dragged his suitcases to the head of the stairs and, without compunction, threw them so that they tumbled roughly to the bottom. She went back, gathered up his books and threw them down the steps, too. Abusing books gave her a momentary qualm, but they were his books, another part of his everlasting lies, so she did it anyway. She took the broken box and marched downstairs.

Alec had heard the noise and awaited her at the foot of the stairs. "Your typical reaction, I see," he said between his teeth. "You feel a passion and throw yourself into it with abandon."

"No," she corrected him. "What I threw were your things. Here are a few more." She reached into the box and threw the copies of her grandfather's documents into the air. "Do you mind telling me why you crept around our attic like a rat? What was this for? Did you hope to find something else my grandfather had done? Treason, perhaps?"

She tossed the broken box away with insulting casualness. She heard it bounce against a stair and break again.

He looked down at her, breathing hard. The muscle in his cheek was pulsing hard. "I knew approximately what the old boy was worth when he left India. I wanted to see if any big influx of money had come in that would mean he'd sold the jewel. But it hadn't—things balanced out. He'd obviously kept it. That's when I knew I'd have to search the house. Do you think I liked any of this?"

"It doesn't matter if you liked it. What matters is you did it," she returned with a toss of her head.

"Listen, Kimberly—" he began, his tone dangerous.

"Kimberly!" Dodo's voice came from upstairs. "Whatever is happening? What are you doing?"

Kimberly wheeled. Her aunt stood at the top of the stairs. She looked pale but held herself erectly. She wore a long blue cotton robe and clutched its lapels tightly together.

Calvin had left the group of men in the living room and came to stand beside Kimberly. "Dodo," he said, his voiced worried. "Shouldn't you be in bed? You should rest."

"I've rested all I can," she answered, starting to descend the stairs. "I've been awake, and I've been thinking. And there's something I must tell Mr. Shaughnessy."

Kimberly flashed Alec a look of passionate indignation, then turned her attention to her aunt. "Don't let him upset you anymore," she entreated.

Dodo reached the bottom of the stairs. "He doesn't upset me, dear," she said softly. Calvin took her elbow and stood by her side, looking down at her with concern.

Dodo stared up at Alec Shaughnessy, pain in her blue eyes. "Mr. Shaughnessy," she murmured, "I was angry and hurt by what you did. I hope you can understand my reaction. And forgive it."

"What?" Kimberly gasped. "You can't apologize to him, Dodo. You can't!"

"Hush, Kimberly," Dodo said firmly. Calvin's face filled with emotion as he looked at the small woman beside him. Dodo kept gazing at Alec with determination.

"My family has apparently done yours a great wrong," she said softly. "I know that no apology of mine can undo that wrong. But I must apologize, and I do. The truth, of course, must be made public. And I want you to know I do not expect you to try to spare my family's feelings. The right thing must be done at last. Please tell your father—" for the first time Dodo faltered, but she went one "—tell your father that I would give my life to undo the harm that has been done. But when I testified against your grandfather, I thought I told the truth."

Alec stared at Dodo in silence for a long moment. "I didn't know you'd be capable of taking it this way, Miss Simpson. But I'd begun to hope you might—someday. That you can do it now shows you're a lady. A very great one, I think."

"No," Dodo replied, her face deeply troubled. "Only a foolish one. From the beginning there were stories of my father's—involvement. I chose not to believe them. Because I loved him. And feared him, too. I knew his temper was terrible, and I tried to always keep him happy, so he wouldn't lash out and hurt someone. Deep in my heart, although I never wanted to admit it, I was afraid he was capable of it. I pretended he wasn't, and that everything was fine—and prayed I was right. It will be no comfort to anyone, but I, too, have paid for what was done. For years I lived a lie—never certain that it was a lie—determined to believe it was not.''

Calvin put his arm around her. She looked weak again, as if she had used up all her strength. ''Come sit down,'' he ordered.

''I understand your feelings,'' she continued, still looking Alec in the eye, ''and what you did, and why. I would even admire you for it, Mr. Shaughnessy, if it were not for what you've done to Kimberly. Justice is worth almost any price, but vengeance—well, vengeance is worth none.''

''Dodo, come sit down,'' Calvin insisted again.

''No,'' she said. ''I must help Mr. Shaughnessy pick up his things.'' She tried to bend over to start picking up the jumbled possessions that Kimberly had thrown.

''No!'' Kimberly cried. ''Sit down—I'll do it. It's my fault, and I'll take care of it.'' Humiliated, she knelt and began gathering up the books. Her heart hammered so hard it nearly choked her. Calvin led Dodo into the kitchen.

''Who are all these people?'' Kimberly heard Dodo ask, bewildered.

Calvin tried to explain.

''Get up,'' Alec commanded. His voice was harsh.

Kimberly refused to look at him.

''Get up!'' Alec practically snarled. He reached down and hauled her to her feet so suddenly that she spilled all the books again.

''Don't touch me!'' she ordered. She backed a step away and stared at him with fury.

''Did I ask you to kneel and pick them up? No. Let them be,'' he said savagely.

"Dodo may forgive you," she said, her dark eyes blazing, "but I never will. Do you know what it must have cost her to say that? I'll hate you until the day I die."

"Will you?" he asked caustically. "Then your grandfather lives on in you—hardheaded, hard-hearted and wrathful. Your aunt is an extraordinary woman. She has made a life of giving, and now, she's given even to me—which proves just how great-hearted she is. I once thought I could see the best of her in you—perhaps I was wrong. At least I understand now—how a man might destroy himself over one of you. I see that clearly."

"What do you mean?" Kimberly asked, her head high.

"My father told me the story," Alec said bitterly. "My grandfather went to India a widower. He had two sons back at school in England. And in India, he and your grandmother fell in love. She would have left the colonel for him, but instead your grandfather destroyed him. Left him a shell."

"That's ridiculous," Kimberly argued, wanting to deny anything he said. "Why should the colonel kill the rajah to frame your grandfather? That makes no sense. The rajah was his friend."

"Yes," said Alec with a cold smile. "Until he fell in love with your aunt."

"My aunt?" Kimberly scoffed in disbelief. "Dodo? She was no more than fourteen when the rajah died. She was a child."

"In India in those days, a girl of fourteen was considered a woman grown. And Dodo, you can't deny, is beautiful, was beautiful—as beautiful as she was unworldly. My grandfather was the first to see the gleam in the rajah's eye. He warned your grandmother, and she told the colonel. He was enraged—he saw two powerful men coveting his women, and he contrived a way to destroy them both."

Kimberly shook her head. "No," she denied. "That's all impossible."

"Is it?" he asked sarcastically. "It was simple, really. Pratap wanted the throne—he cooperated willingly. Servants are easy to bribe. All that was needed was one unimpeachable witness who could testify that Sir Cyril was seen coming from the gem room after the murder. And the colonel arranged that, too."

"Dodo?" Kimberly protested. "Dodo would never lie about anything—especially anything important. She *saw* Sir Cyril come out of that room. She swore to it in court."

"She saw someone in my grandfather's uniform come out of that room, Kimberly. Sir Cyril always claimed to have missed the appointment. He said he'd fallen asleep—drugged, probably. The colonel arranged to have Dodo arrive at the gem room just in time to see someone—one of the servants, most likely—come out. You know her eyes are bad. All that registered was the uniform. But that was enough to put my grandfather in disgrace until his dying day."

Kimberly looked away. She could no longer meet his accusing gaze. What he said contained a horrible sort of logic. And poor Dodo, she thought—never knowing she had excited the secret desire of the ruthless rajah. Or that she had been used by her equally ruthless father. There was one thing Kimberly could do for her—protect her from the ugliest facts, at least.

Alec watched the guilt and anguish play across her face. "If she wonders," he said, as if reading her mind, "tell her the three of them quarreled about the fate of the Heart of the Sun. That's true enough. Sir Cyril wanted it turned over to the crown, the rajah wanted it cut in the Western way, and your grandfather wanted it kept as it was. Well, he got his wish—for a while. But there's no reason to hang out all the dirty linen of both families. Let the old, forbidden loves stay secret.''

"Forbidden loves," Kimberly echoed biting. "Yes. You've already got in your blow at the forbidden loves.''

He glared at her, nostrils flaring. He acted as if he hadn't heard her. "You can also tell your aunt that she may have testified against my grandfather, but she also saved him from hanging. She was so frightened, so easily confused by the attorneys, and so honest about her confusion that her testimony was worthless. That part of your grandfather's plan didn't work. For her sake, I'll keep your family name out of this as much as possible. The important thing is the gem is recovered. And the Damon name is cleared. My father can go home to England. He knows. I've called. My brother is preparing to take him."

One of the state policemen, solemn-faced, stepped into the hallway. "We've got the thing removed, Shaughnessy," he said. "We're going. I'll need you to come along. I want you to sign another statement about this thing."

"Of course," Alec said. "I need to pick up this rubbish, first." He bent and retrieved the two parts of the broken box.

"Here," said the stonemason, joining them. "I'll give you a hand." He began gathering up the scattered books.

Alec straightened, lifting a suitcase. He threw Kimberly a piercing look. "Australia's a big country. But a determined woman could find me there if she wanted to."

"I don't want to," she said between her teeth. "You're right. I'm not like my aunt. I can't forgive you. You've cleared your name. But ruined her."

The silence between them was so charged it almost threw off sparks. "Then I have only one question for you. If our positions were reversed—if it were Dodo dying and homesick in Australia, wouldn't you have come here to do what I've done?''

She looked at him, sick with churning emotions. "No," she said sharply. "Never." But she knew better. If their positions had been reversed she would have done almost exactly the same. But he shouldn't have pretended to love her. That had been cruel beyond words. "Never," she whispered again, her voice full of censure.

"I see," he said. "I guess it's goodbye, then." He picked up his other suitcase. It had a shoulder strap, and he slipped it over one arm. "I'll be at the Basin Park Hotel until tomorrow if you change your mind."

She could not bear to watch him go. She turned and fled upstairs. She heard the clatter of slamming car doors outside. To drown it out she threw herself on the bed and buried her burning face in the pillow.

There had been a time when she had thought her aunt weak, even silly, but now Kimberly feared she didn't have half of Dodo's strength. She could never find it in her heart to forgive Alec Shaughnessy—for anything—for even the smallest of his lies.

He had stripped away any semblance of respectability her family had left. He had destroyed Dodo's illusions. He had made love to Kimberly for reasons she couldn't begin to understand, and he had never even tried to explain himself. It was as if he had come to her family, like a curse incarnate, stalking them across the years. He had come to do battle with her grandfather's ghost, he had used every weapon at his disposal, and he had won.

Her grandfather's ghost, she thought emptily. Ghosts and curses and prophecies. What had been Alec's rhyming charm?

A gift, a ghost, a friend, a foe,
A letter to come, a journey to go.

It had all come true now. There had been a gift, more than one. There had been the ghost of her grandfather's wrong, haunting them for all these years. A friend—Calvin, and a foe—Alec himself. Even a letter and finally a journey. For Alec had what he had come for, and he was going away forever now.

She wished she could cry, but she was too exhausted. And something nagged at her mind. The letter, she thought at last. The letter. She hadn't opened the letter from her mother.

She propped herself up on her elbow. She reached into her pocket and drew out the envelope. It was crumpled. She opened it and took out the folded sheets. At first she was too numb and shocked to care what it said. Then the words and sentences began to sink into her mind.

Her mother's letter began by wishing her a happy twenty-first birthday and telling her solemnly that Kimberly was officially an adult now, old enough to know the truth and know how powerful it was.

And then, the letter told a story. It was much the same one that Alec had told her so short a time before. It was a story of desire and jealousy, love and betrayal.

Once again Kimberly was immersed in the old story that had played itself out in India so many years ago. But it was the close of her mother's letter that shook her to the very core:

I have hated the colonel at times. I have blamed him—and others—for any number of things. But Kimberly, as I realize that I will not live long, I also realize that the two most wasteful things in life are hate and blame.

The colonel, not I, will see you grow up. He is a deeply unhappy man, Kimberly, and in his way, perhaps has paid for all the wrong he's done. I don't think he has ever had one truly peaceful or joyful moment. What he has done to everyone is unforgivable, but what he has done to himself is unspeakable. If we are to save ourselves from being the same as he is, we must forgive him.

Dodo will take care of you. Learn from her. I used to resent her and think I was so much wiser, being so much more bitter. But she has the goodness that comes only from real innocence, and she has loved us with all her heart. She is the only person I know who has the true gift of forgiveness. If she could teach you only one thing, I wish she'd teach you that.

I pray that you will live well and fully. I pray that you, too, will love with all your heart. And I pray that you learn never to hate. We are here on this beautiful earth for so short a time, it does not do to spend any of it in bitterness. I love you.

Your mother,
Margaret Simpson Dodge

Kimberly sat on the edge of the bed, her back very straight, and read the letter again. She read it a third time. The tears she hadn't been able to shed when Alec left burned in her eyes.

She rose and went to her window. She didn't know how long she'd been in her room. Now it was almost dusk. The late-afternoon air was still and suffused with gold. Shadows were long.

All right, she said to herself, trying to keep her back straight and her chin high. All right. *I don't hate him. I love him. And I think he loves me.* Because no matter what had been said or done today, every time he looked at her, she still believed they loved each other.

And if he loves me, he'll come back. He'd know she couldn't go to him, because it would hurt too much. So he'd come back.

She sat on the edge of the bed again, staring out the window, unseeing. The sky turned a deeper gold, then lavender gray, then slowly it became black.

Calvin came and knocked at her door, asking if she was all right. She said she was. Later, Dodo came and asked the same question. Again Kimberly said she was all right. She didn't know if she was or not. She simply sat and waited. She felt as if her soul was in the balance. By this time tomorrow, she would have learned her mother's lesson, or she would never be able to learn it as long as she lived. For now, she could only wait.

The sky had been black for what seemed like a long time, when Dodo knocked timidly at the door again. "Kimberly," she said in her breathless little voice, "I don't know what to do. Alec's here. He insists on seeing you. Do you want me to send him away?"

Numbly Kimberly rose and opened the door. She looked into Dodo's large, troubled eyes.

"Calvin will make him go, if you want," Dodo said. "But somehow, I have a feeling that you ought to see him, Kimberly. There's something in his face, in his eyes that's so— so lost. Oh, I don't know what to say."

"I'll see him," Kimberly replied tonelessly. Her throat felt dry, her knees undependable.

"He's out in back," Dodo said worriedly. "Waiting in the garden. Kimberly, are you all right? You look lost yourself. Like a pale little ghost."

Kimberly reached out and took her aunt by the hand. Together they walked down the stairs. *I need your strength,* Kimberly thought, feeling frightened and empty. Dodo

squeezed her hand as if to say, *Then you have it all. It's
yours.*

At the foot of the stairs Dodo turned to her. "In India, a
holy man once told me that often the old forms have to be
destroyed in order for new, strong ones to be created. He
said this sort of destruction was good. I didn't understand
then. I think I do now. Mr. Shaughnessy has destroyed
much of the old. I think it needed destroying. I'm not afraid
to let go of the old, dear. And you mustn't be afraid to face
the new. Either of you. Whatever it holds."

Calvin stood in the kitchen, his face dark with confusion
and concern. "Kimberly," he began, "if you don't want to
see him—"

"She does," Dodo affirmed. "I can see she does. Go to
him, dear."

Kimberly stepped out onto the stones of the little back
porch. The moon hung low, and the stars were thick and
glittering. She saw him. He stood, a tall shadowy figure by
the catalpa tree.

She walked toward him slowly. A breeze had come up and
fluttered her hair.

"My aunt," she said to the dark figure, her voice almost
quivering, "said you wanted to see me."

She stood before him now, and he stared down at her for
a long time. Kimberly felt as many kinds of apprehension as
there were stars in the sky. What was he going to say? What
could he say, or she either for that matter?

He said nothing. Instead he suddenly took her in his arms
and pulled her so tightly against him that she sobbed for
breath. His own breath was labored. She could feel the ragged rise and fall of his chest.

Her arms wrapped around him as if by enchantment. It
seemed they belonged nowhere else. She clung to him so
hard that it hurt. Her face was pressed against his chest, and

his lips were on her hair, and then on her forehead. One of his hands tipped her face up to his, and then his mouth was on hers in a kiss that dizzied her.

"I can't leave you," he said, his hand on her throat. He breathed the words fervently against her lips. "I won't leave you. I'll die before I leave you." Emotion choked his voice.

He kissed her again. His touch communicated all the ferocious complexity of his feelings. It was as if the two of them were caught in the storm again, only this time the storm was more immense. It was a force as old as India, as old as stones, as old as the stars in the sky.

"I didn't know," he muttered between his teeth, "until I met you I didn't know." He nipped at her lower lip as if he would find it sweet to devour her. He kissed her, then pulled her close, speaking against her hair. "I didn't know what it was like—to want someone so that it was a fire in the blood every hour in the day. To love them so much it was like—like nothing ever described, nothing that could be described. I love you, Kimberly."

He drew back, his breath almost panting. "How could I know when I came here that the price of that cursed jewel might be you? How many times must it twist and destroy? Tell me that we can escape and love each other. Tell me that you can forgive me. And that you love me. Because I thought I still saw it in your face today. That you loved me. Despite the long years of enmity between our families. Despite all the anger and pain."

"I—" Kimberly began, her voice strangled. "I've never been able to understand what you felt, but somehow I believed—"

She could not finish her sentence. What she felt was too complicated and powerful to utter. "Believe this, love," he said and kissed her again. His arms around her were both possessive and protective. "Tell me you'll come with me. Back to Australia," he demanded.

"You said I couldn't," she protested, puzzled yet filling with joy.

He shook his head. "Before, I thought my father wouldn't be able to accept it," he explained, his voice taut. "It doesn't matter now. He's going back to England, and the old hates have to die. His, too. They all must. They've never caused anything but grief. And they've caused enough."

She looked up at him, blinking hard. In the starlight, her tears made him look as if he were surrounded by blurry diamonds.

"Kimberly," he said harshly, his face close to hers, "I wanted you so much that I had to swear an oath not to have you wrongly. I prayed the stupid gem wouldn't be here, that you'd never know why I'd come. That I could go home and then come back to you... start again. Then I found it, and I was afraid of losing you. I wanted to marry you. Then you'd be bound to me, and no matter what happened about the jewel, you couldn't be quit of me. Not easily, you couldn't."

"That's why you wanted to marry me?"

"I swear," he vowed. "Once I found the thing, I knew I'd have to hurt you—both you and your aunt. But if you married me, I thought—you'd be bound to me. Perhaps I could make you believe how much I loved you."

"Alec," she breathed, "I almost went with you last night."

"If you had," he replied, lacing his fingers in her hair near her temples, "then I might have tried to explain this muddle."

"What you said was true," she offered, putting her hand up to touch his lips. "There was a letter from my mother—

she wrote it for my twenty-first birthday—I just read it. She said the same thing as you. You can have it. Show it to your father. To whoever needs to see it.''

"Kimberly, that's incredibly generous. That's beautiful of you, love.''

"And I lied,'' she declared. "I would have done what you did—for Dodo. I would have had to.''

"It tore me in two, Kimberly, knowing he was dying back in Perth—then to fall in love with you and know that, to ensure his happiness, I'd have to steal yours.''

"My mother wrote,'' Kimberly whispered, "that I should never hate or blame, that love was more important—''

"Then she was wise,'' he assured her solemnly, drinking in the love in her eyes. "So tell me that you can forgive me. That you still love me. That you'll come back home with me.''

"I forgive you,'' she murmured happily. "I love you. I'll go anywhere with you.''

"And say you'll marry me as soon as possible—I have to know you're mine. And will be. Always.''

"I will,'' she nodded. "Always.''

"It'll be an odd life,'' he said, half-smiling. "You may find yourself in a tent in the outback, watching me shoot footage of dingoes. Or the rock art in Kakadu. Events may take us strange places, love.''

"If I study hard, will you let me storyboard for you?''

"I don't know. Are you one of those temperamental artists?''

"I'm afraid so.''

"So am I. Good. We'll understand each other.''

She gazed up happily at the expression in his face. She had seen that look before and wondered if she understood it. Now she knew that she'd read it rightly. It was love, and it was real.

He kissed her again. The dark leaves danced in the starlight, and Kimberly's heart danced with them.

INSIDE THE HOUSE Dodo was trying to peek discreetly out the window. "Oh, Calvin," she said, squinting in frustration at the darkness. "I shouldn't look, but I can't stand it, and I can't see a thing. What do you think is happening?"

Calvin peered out into the starry night, saw the forms beneath the catalpa tree. He took the curtain from Dodo's fingers and let it drop back into place. He shook his head. He wasn't sure he'd ever understand women. But he supposed he'd spend the rest of his life trying. "I can't believe this," he said, shaking his head. "I think they've made up."

"Really?" Dodo asked, looking up at him.

He put his arm around her. She seemed happy with the news, so it must be all right. He nodded and walked her into the front room.

"Really?" she repeated.

"Really," he said, and kissed her.

"Good," she said. She gazed thoughtfully at the ruined fireplace. "Good. It's time for old things to be done with. And new things to begin."

"Yes." He smiled, holding her near. He was a lucky man. His heart flooded with pleasure and love. "It's time."

Coming Next Month

#3049 ANOTHER TIME, ANOTHER LOVE Anne Beaumont
Laurel Curtis isn't planning to change her status as a single mother. A traumatic experience with one man was enough. Connor Dyson, an Australian property tycoon buying the lease on her flat, has other ideas—like taking over Laurel, too!

#3050 PARTNERS IN PASSION Rosemary Carter
Teri comes back to her grandfather's African game farm where eight years ago, before she had to move with her parents, she had loved Rafe—and thought he loved her, too. Now Rafe greets her as a stranger.

#3051 · FACE VALUE Rosemary Hammond
Christine agrees to do one last modeling job before she changes careers. John Falconer, however, has devised the assignment of a commercial for his company simply to meet her—and he offers Chris another proposition entirely.

#3052 HOME FOR LOVE Ellen James
When interior designer Kate Melrose is hired to redecorate an unknown client's home, she falls instantly in love—with the house! But she soon falls even harder for its owner, the handsome, irascible Steven Reid.

#3053 THE CHAIN OF DESTINY Betty Neels
When Guy Bowers-Bentinck comes to her rescue, Suzannah, alone in the world and without a job, is forced to accept his help. Not that she wants to be beholden to such an infuriatingly arrogant man!

#3054 RASH CONTRACT Angela Wells
Karis doesn't welcome the reappearance of Nik Christianides in her life—reawakening tragic memories she's spent years trying to suppress. Now, though, she has to listen to him because he has a way of replacing what she had lost.

Available in May wherever paperback books are sold, or through Harlequin Reader Service:

In the U.S.
901 Fuhrmann Blvd.
P.O. Box 1397
Buffalo, N.Y. 14240-1397

In Canada
P.O. Box 603
Fort Erie, Ontario
L2A 5X3

M